One Little Lie

by

EJ Towler

One Little Lie

Cover Art by *Kristian Norris*

The Wild Rose Press, Inc.
PO Box 708
Adams Basin, NY 14410-0708
Visit us at www.thewildrosepress.com

Publishing History
First Edition, 2023
Trade Paperback ISBN 978-1-5092-4566-6
Digital ISBN 978-1-5092-4567-3

Published in the United States of America

JD turned slowly in front of the trifold mirror. The black, floor-length, Austrian bobbin lace gown molded to her curves. She wasn't sure what bothered her most: the plunging neckline barely keeping her breasts in place, the nonexistent back, or the front scalloped lace slit that damn near showed what Wendi called her fine china. At least the onyx pearl silk lining was almost the length of the miniskirts she'd worn as a teenager.

"Let's add the mask," Suzie the tailor said, her voice almost giddy.

JD watched herself disappear behind the black crocheted mask. The iridescent shades of the blue and black peacock feathers framed the left side. A diamond pin held the plume in place.

"You look amazing. I think this is my best work ever," Suzie said as she broke into a wide, open smile.

The mask secured, JD looked in the mirror, and the reflection was unrecognizable. A soft gasp of relief escaped her lips. No one would know it was her behind the mask. Now all she had to do was find the courage to walk downstairs with Mitch. Her body tingled with excitement and nerves.

As if he'd read her mind, Mitch peered over her shoulder. They were alone. She hadn't seen Suzie leave. His eyes were compelling, almost magnetic.

When he didn't speak, she said, using the deep southern accent she'd practiced over the last two weeks, "Well, do I look okay? It's the mask. The feathers have to go, right?"

Praise for EJ Towler

Previous release Stealth Maneuvers.

One Little Lie—first three chapters won second place in Finish The Damn Book Contest by Chesapeake Romance Writers.

Dedication

One Little Lie is dedicated to the people who encouraged me to write again: my sister, husband, friends, fans, and Joy Lezon, the person who dared me to dream in the first place. Some of the names have been changed to protect the not so innocent; you know who you are.

Prologue

Tallahassee, Florida
February 2000

Detective MacWilliams' stomach twisted at the sight of the young woman tied to the bed. There didn't appear to be a place on her small frame that hadn't been mutilated. The silk neckties restraining her were saturated with blood from the small cuts to her ankles, feet, and wrists. The stabs appeared deeper and more frenzied moving up the body as if the killer had been creating some macabre masterpiece. She'd almost been decapitated by the jagged cut from ear to ear.

The four-poster bed was soaked with a clear outline of the body and that of a person who'd been lying beside her. The detective had been on the job long enough to know the cast-off blood splatter showed the woman had been stabbed by someone beside her. He scratched the back of his neck. Why couldn't this have happened one mile down the road—not in his jurisdiction?

This was going to be crazier than a three-ring circus, and the job of ringmaster had landed in his lap. The murder was bad enough—a woman found tied to a bed all but butchered; the media would be all over this. He surveyed the sex toys on the dresser, a continuation of what he'd found in what appeared to be a toolbox. Some of those items he had no idea what they were, much less used for. This would call for serious research; it would be funny if not for the situation. Glancing at the body, guilt and frustration snaked down his spine. This wasn't about him.

It was time to deal with the man found covered in blood: James Derrick August, multi-millionaire, crusader of the needy and downtrodden. He had friends in high places; everyone who was anybody knew him. Hell, he could've probably been elected governor, but rumor had it he didn't have the stomach for politics. However, it appears he had an appetite for another vice.

MacWilliams blew out a deep breath, surveyed the group of crime scene techs methodically documenting the room, and turned his attention to the man soaked in blood, who claimed he was innocent. He'd heard it all over the years. This had to be good. He needed to speak with Mr. August before his army of lawyers descended like beaching Normandy.

Chapter One

February 2000

JD woke before the blare of the alarm, snuggled beneath the covers, stretching like a lazy cat. The warmth of the electric blanket against her nude body was heavenly. Well, she was naked except for the wool dachshund-printed socks and engagement ring. Nestling in the lavish, platform, king-size bed, she held up her hand and moved it side to side. The flames from the stone fireplace danced through the three-carat emerald cut diamond.

The aroma of brewing coffee beckoned from the kitchen, but she decided to be lazy and stay put until Derrick's morning call. The erotic beginning of their day would be sensual banter ending in phone sex, in which JD would be a willing participant. It was their guilty pleasure when he traveled, which had been a great deal lately. *It's part of our strategic life plan,* she heard Derrick's voice remind her.

She tickled the snout of the stuffed dog on her nightstand. One day she'd have a dachshund who'd be her constant companion. She'd wanted a wiener dog for as long as she could remember. Being all but homeless much of her childhood, finding food and staying safe had been her primary focus. The streets were no place for a pet, and now she was consumed with setting up a law career. Derrick was right, as usual; their lives were too hectic for a puppy. Another topic on the long list of controversial subjects he reluctantly agreed to revisit in a few years.

JD mentally scolded herself again, *don't dwell on the past or things you can't have. Nothing positive comes from reliving the past.* Besides, the only homeless shelter she'd entered in years had been to volunteer. Since she met Derrick, her life was nothing short of a fairy tale; overnight, she'd gone from living paycheck to paycheck to private jets and limos.

Now her dream wedding was in the works. The coordinator had mailed the save-the-date cards months ago. The invitations would go out in a few days, exactly eight weeks before the celebration. Their union would be the social event of the season. JD rested against the pile of pillows and stared at her ring.

She shook her head, recalling how they'd flown to New York City, met with a designer, and spent thirty-five thousand dollars on dresses. She tried on several styles until he decided the fit and flare style was sexy and tasteful. He left JD in the hands of the artist.

The final drawing detailed the white illusion bodice and fingertip sleeves, plunging V back, and a long double lace train. With the floating lace motifs, decadent overlays, shimmery lace, and embellishments, the dress would be unforgettable. In stark contrast, Derrick selected a red reception gown for her. To go with each, hidden away in her closet were two lace-up corsets, one white and the other red with hoses and heels.

What had she been thinking? Oh, she knew, all too well, over the last several years, she'd become way too comfortable in Derrick's world. Hadn't she spent nine hundred dollars on a pair of heels last week without a second thought? Her closet was filled with everything an up-and-coming professional required.

JD owed Derrick everything; he believed in her when there had been no one else. She'd been a struggling college student working in a video store when they met. He'd come in looking for a copy of *Casablanca* and had taken her breath away. Chills danced down her spine as she recalled the encounter.

The classic wool suit fit perfectly to his tall, muscular frame, yet he reminded her of a teddy bear. The blue shirt set off the crystal color of his eyes, and a glint of gold sparkled from his cuff links. He'd unbuttoned his jacket and revealed button suspenders that matched the manatee and coral tie.

Her life had changed forever that day. Within weeks, at Derrick's insistence, she quit her job and moved into his house on Lake Ella. She was his princess, free to concentrate on her education. With his direction, they put together an amazing wardrobe. She hadn't known there were so many designers of women's clothing. *One must wear designer suits, good fabric, and good cuts.* JD could hear Derrick's voice as if he was standing in front of her.

Derrick taught her to work a room and host the perfect party. Introduced her to a world she never dreamed existed, and challenged her to apply for law school while finishing her bachelor's degree. All the while, his money and connections paved the way for her new life.

When she graduated from law school, he'd thrown a huge party and bragged to anyone who'd listen how she finished first in her class. JD was sure Derrick was the driving force in her landing a summer internship at Dewey, Cheatam, and Howe, Esquires. It had been her strong work ethic and judicial success that had her on the fast track toward partner, but still, if not for Derrick, where would she be?

His circle of friends had welcomed her with open arms. The four were so alike yet vastly different. JD recalled the series of pictures on the piano downstairs documenting Derrick, Johnathan, Benjamin, and Mitch's relationship over the years. They were closer than any family by blood.

Johnathan and Benjamin were now her bosses. JD counted Mitch, restaurateur and entrepreneur, as a best friend. Over the years, each had contributed to her personal and professional growth and held a special place in her heart.

The ring of her phone sent tingles of anticipation through JD's body, and a smile spread across her face. So, now the fun begins.

JD hit the speaker button. "Good morning, my love." She let the words roll out in the sweet, southern drawl her fiancé loved and she only used for him.

"Sweetheart, I think I'm going to be arrested!" Derrick's voice boomed in her ears.

The tremble in his voice told her this wasn't one of his infamous practical jokes. She shot up and swung her feet over the side of the bed. The dump of adrenaline set her heart pounding. She fought to control her breathing and finally found her voice. "Arrested? Arrested for what?"

"Murder."

"Murder! Who the hell did you allegedly murder?" Terror began to take hold, and she consciously shifted from fiancée to attorney. She cloaked herself in the cold legal persona she'd mastered.

JD threw the phone on the bed, and slipped a T-shirt over her head. "Never mind. Where are you?" she asked and pulled on sweatpants.

There was a pause and a deep breath before Derrick answered. "At the cottage."

JD retrieved her cell and began to pace. Her sock-covered feet moved smoothly across the high polished Bocate wood floors. "Our cabin? I thought you were in Tampa."

"There was a change of plans."

She heard the defeat in his voice as she ran her fingers through her hair. "All right, we'll talk about that later. Have you been read your rights?"

"No. The detective told me to sit and wait. What do I do?"

"Make one statement; you want your attorney. Don't say another word, not one. Understand?" she said, forcing calm into her voice.

"Okay."

"Who's the detective in charge?" she asked.

"MacWilliams, I think, wait, he's heading this way."

JD took her first deep breath since the call began. "Inform him you're speaking with your attorney, and I'd like to speak with him." Oh yeah, she'd talk to him. She'd worked with Mac before. Well, more like against him. On numerous occasions, she'd ripped his evidence to shreds defending her clients, but in most cases, Mac was right.

She listened to the muffled sounds until a familiar male voice echoed through the phone. "This is Detective MacWilliams. I really don't have time to talk, especially to an attorney."

"Mac, it's JD."

"Wow, I'm impressed. This guy must have you on speed dial to reach you at this hour. I figured it wasn't his first rodeo."

"I understand you're busy. I have two questions," JD said, mentally shutting down the alarm bells clanging in her head. In some cases, Mac was an excellent detective.

"Only two questions. Must mean there'll be follow-ups?"

Sarcasm dripped from each word. She could visualize the smirk on the detective's face as she asked, "Is Mr. August being taken into custody?"

His response was quick and direct. "Yes."

"Is he being transported to Tallahassee Police headquarters?"

"Correct again, Counselor. You are two for two. Want to try for the hat trick?" he asked.

"I'll meet you at the station. Consider this notification Mr. August has evoked his right to counsel. He'll make no statements."

"What is it, JD? You don't trust me?"

The mockery rang loud and clear in his voice. JD paused for a split second, then responded in kind, "I've beaten you before, haven't I? Remember this isn't our first dance, Mac."

"This one's nothing like the others," he replied flatly.

"JD—" It was Derrick now.

"Derrick, shut up!" Panic was breaking through her mental castle walls.

"Not a word. Do you hear me? Say nothing, do

nothing." She didn't wait for a response, just disconnected the call. It could all be explained. It had to be. But in the back of her mind, an old familiar voice whispered, *You knew things were too good to be true.*

JD's stomach churned, and the room began to spin. She sat on the bed, put her head between her knees, and fought to breathe. She had to find her inner calm; panic would solve nothing. She raised her head and tried to dismiss the dread invading her mind, body, and heart.

What the hell was going on? Why hadn't Derrick gone to Tampa like he said? Did Mac suspect Derrick had murdered someone or that an intruder had broken into the cabin? She shut down the thoughts swirling in her mind, stripped, and stepped into the shower.

****

JD selected a suit bag from the closet. Derrick had insisted each tailored, designer suit, coordinated blouse, and perfect pair of heels be placed in their own bag. That way, she'd never waste time putting outfits together; they were always ready to go. Today, that was certainly true, no thought necessary.

She slipped into the silk Guia La Bruna knickers and bra, pushing down her thoughts. Better no thoughts at all than dwell on the current situation. She'd handle this however it played out. JD blanked her mind and dressed.

She turned in the mirror and checked her appearance from top to bottom. Perfection, from the navy suit to the red heels that matched her blouse. Her long dark-brown curls were braided and pinned in a perfect bun at the nape of her neck. A slight dust of brown-and-gray eye shadow highlighted her hazel eyes. Small pearl earrings and a gold pendant watch almost completed the picture.

Even now, when she should hurry and throw on

whatever, Derrick's words slowed her preparation. He drilled into her never to leave the house until she was perfect. She never knew who she might see or what opportunity might present itself.

With confidence, she added red lipstick and slipped the horn-rimmed glasses into place. They were of no practical use. Her vision was twenty-twenty, simply another layer to the character Derrick had helped her create and hone.

Maybe it was some naughty-teacher or sexy-librarian fantasy men shared. She'd never figured it out, but there was something about a woman in glasses. The good old boy lawyers and judges in the South fell for them every time. JD took a deep breath, picked up her briefcase, and headed for the door. Time to evaluate and formulate a plan of attack.

****

As JD turned onto Monroe Street, she mentally checked the day's schedule. Anything to stop the churning in her stomach. Her paralegal, Wendi, wouldn't be surprised when her phone rang at six forty-five. The pair had an understanding. Wendi was available twenty-four seven, and JD made sure her assistant's salary matched the commitment. Their call was short. Wendi would reschedule the appointments for the day. JD would check in when she could.

Her next call was to Johnathan Howe III, grandson of one of the founding partners of the firm. "Good morning, boss," JD said as she navigated traffic.

"Good morning. You beat me to the office again?" His laughter came through in his voice.

JD could tell by his increased breathing she'd caught him in his midmorning run. She steeled her voice before she spoke. "No. I have a situation. Derrick's been taken into custody in connection with a murder."

"What the hell? Derrick. Your Derrick? You have to be kidding."

"No. Detective MacWilliams is the lead; there must be something. He wouldn't take anyone in without damn good probable cause, especially someone like Derrick," she said, checking her mirrors as she changed lanes.

"You want me to meet you at the station?" Johnathan asked.

"No. Just wanted you in the loop."

"I'm about two miles from home. When I get back, I'll do some digging," Johnathan said.

"Thanks." JD ended the call and increased the volume of the stereo. "Hotel California" blared from the speakers. Not Derrick's classical mix but her favorite old rock and roll. She'd have to wait and see what the situation revealed to decide her next move. Her attorney senses were on overdrive, telling her the worst was yet to come.

Chapter Two

As a criminal defense attorney, JD was familiar with TPD headquarters. Leon County was her home court, and she was the rising star. She'd been practicing law for a short time but already had a reputation. Good for the criminals, not so much for the police.

She believed everyone was innocent until proven guilty, and generally, the police and prosecutors got it wrong. They went for the easy answer; investigations were done to prove their predetermined outcome, the truth be dammed.

To say the state prosecutor didn't care for her was an understatement. In the last three years, JD'd made her look foolish in court and on social media. Last year, six defendants who'd been railroaded through the system were found innocent at trial. To add insult to injury, her firm's investigators found the guilty parties. To JD's delight, the outcome left the prosecutor with more than one huge black eye.

JD also understood many of her opponents and colleagues called her a stone-cold bitch behind her back. She smiled at the thought as she checked her makeup in the rearview mirror. JD gave her all when standing for a client; this case would be no exception.

****

JD found Detective MacWilliams at his desk, playing with a blue rubber ball. Derrick sat in a metal chair to his left, handcuffed and dressed in an orange jumpsuit.

She walked to the desk and, without any pleasantries, asked in rapid succession, "Is my client under arrest? What's with the cuffs and jumpsuit? Has Mr. August been charged with a crime?" JD saw Derrick's right hand was bandaged, but didn't mention it.

"Well, good morning to you too. I was just about ready to remove the cuffs," Mac said, standing and expertly unlocking the metal bracelets. "Mr. August hasn't been officially charged. He was taken into custody on a probable cause warrant and voluntarily surrendered his clothing. The jumpsuit was all I had." He shrugged his shoulders before adding, "We're all out of Armani."

JD looked over the top of her glasses. "You're so kind." Her eyes never left the detective's. She put her hand on Derrick's shoulder and whispered, "You okay?"

"I guess." His response was almost unheard above the precinct noise.

She returned her attention to Mac. "Did Mr. August waive his right to counsel?"

"No. I asked if he wanted to change his clothes; his were soiled." Mac tossed a ball in the air and caught it.

His face was too smug. JD wanted to slap him. Instead, she asked, "Soiled with what?" JD cooled her anger and continued the banter. *They'd taken his clothing. The question was, why?*

Mac sat and leaned back, the fingertips of both hands together. "Well, we weren't exactly sure. Like I said, I was trying to be helpful."

"Mac, the last time you were helpful—"

JD was interrupted by a young lady carrying a

medical bag. "I'm here to fingerprint and collect DNA samples of Derrick Thomas August," she said, glancing at the paper she was holding.

"You have a warrant?" JD asked the small lady.

The technician didn't speak, just looked at the detective.

JD returned her stare to Mac. "Well, do you? Either you do, or you don't. It's a simple question."

"It's on the way," the detective admitted.

JD raised her eyebrows and fought back a grin. "See, was that so hard, Mac? I want to speak with my client in private." More to make him squirm than anything else, she asked again, "Is Mr. August under arrest?" JD read frustration on his face.

"He's not been charged, but he can't leave."

"Mac, did you forget your donuts this morning? Either charge him, or we're out of here."

After a long sigh, he stood and held out his hands. "Come on, JD, quit busting my balls. Talk to him in our conference room."

"Just for you," she said and flashed a fake smile. "About the conference room, I gather you'll turn off cameras and recording equipment. No lip-readers in the wings?" She knew her tone oozed with suspicion.

"Room's all yours." Mac pointed toward a room on the left.

"Thanks, Mac. You are a true gentleman." JD raised her hand in a salute.

She gave Derrick a small case and directed him to the bathroom. She sat on a bench while he changed, and used the time to listen. Police could be very chatty when they thought no one was paying attention. Today everyone seemed very tight-lipped.

Derrick returned dressed in jeans and a button-down, blue oxford shirt. As usual, he looked like he'd just stepped out of the latest edition of *Gentlemen's Quarterly*. Although, it was the first time she could recall his face looking drawn and tired. Dark circles ringed his eyes. She led him to the conference room and closed the door. "Tell me what happened. Why, specifically, do they want your blood and DNA?"

"I'm sorry," Derrick said and dropped into a chair at the oval table.

"Screw sorry. Tell me what happened," JD demanded, leaning in and placing her palms on the table.

Derrick stared past her and whispered, "I don't want to hurt you."

"Something happened. Unless I know the truth, I can't help you. Forget who I am; tell your attorney what happened."

After a long pause, he began, his voice low and monotone. "There's a part of my life you know nothing about; I love you."

It seemed the "I love you" was for effect, not because he meant it. "Stop the bullshit and tell me. I didn't think you ever had trouble talking to me. I need the facts and fast. Who is it they think you killed, and why?"

"Her name is Megan Ferguson. We met online and planned to spend last night together."

JD's heart was pounding. Confusion clouded her mind. She mentally counted to ten, surrounding herself with her legal coat of armor. She'd face the situation with the persona that had served well many times in the past. "Go on with it, be a man, grow a pair!"

Derrick looked up with fire in his eyes. He was

angry. Her ploy had worked.

"Megan and I were into sadism and masochism. We were going to have some fun." His hot glare faded with each syllable.

"Go on," JD said and diverted her eyes to gain control over the anger and dread. Personally, she wanted to slap him and yell, "Shut up!" Professionally, she had no choice but to keep going. It was her role she'd chosen.

"We were getting to know each other, drinking wine. I tied her to the bed. Then it all goes blank until banging on the door woke me. I was lying next to her on the bed. There was blood everywhere, Megan was covered in it, and I was holding a knife."

He ran his hands through his hair. "I didn't. I know I didn't kill her. Someone's setting me up. Maybe I was drugged. Shit, I'm in real trouble, aren't I?"

JD tried to read his eyes but saw only stark, vivid fear. A gut-wrenching silence passed between them. "What happened to your hand?"

"I don't know. There were cuts on my palm. An EMT bandaged it." Derrick turned his hand over and examined the dressing.

"Did you have sex with her?" JD forced herself to make eye contact. It was difficult to swallow; movies of Derrick with other women played in her mind.

"No. I don't think so," Derrick mumbled.

"Okay, stop right there." JD held up her hands. "We're going to volunteer your blood and DNA. State Attorney Phore will issue the warrant anyway. Don't say a word. Do you understand?"

"What about us?"

"We'll cross that bridge when we are *really* alone. At this point, nothing else matters." *Should I believe he*

16

loves me? How can I trust anything he says? Obviously, he's a consummate liar, but how long has he been lying? JD swallowed the bitter taste in her mouth and headed to the door.

She exited the room and motioned to Mac. "Give me ten minutes, and Mr. August will voluntarily provide his fingerprints, blood, and DNA." JD stopped Mac and the technician outside the conference room. "No questions, Mac, understand? I'll be back to witness the collection of evidence."

"I got it, JD, no questions." He placed his hands in his pockets and appeared to be kicking dirt with his shoes like a little boy caught with his hand in the cookie jar.

JD headed to the exit. She wanted to run but forced her legs to move deliberately. Her heart refused to hear what her mind was screaming. Her body was assaulting itself. Her heart thundered in her ears, her shoulder muscles were like rocks, and her flight response was in overdrive. She had to escape, if only for a second, and find a place to breathe. She made it outside to the railing before her stomach wrenched and emptied the yellow, liquid bile onto the boxwoods below. She fought back rolling nausea and wiped the last of the sick with the back of her hand.

****

JD leaned against a wrought iron railing and fought the waves of nausea. Tears swam in her eyes. How could she represent Derrick when he'd gut-punched her? How many more lies would she uncover?

There was no changing the situation. She closed her eyes, wiped the tears from her cheeks, removed the phone from her pocket, and dialed. Johnathan answered on the first ring.

"What do you need?" was all he asked.

"You ASAP. It's bad." She realized she'd shifted into automatic pilot; this was good.

"For once, I'm a step ahead of you. I spoke with a friend in the police chief's office. Decided you'd need the full team like yesterday. Has Derrick been charged?"

"No. But it won't be long. They took him into custody on a probable cause warrant." She walked in circles as she spoke.

"What's first on your list?" Johnathan's voice seemed far away.

JD mentally shook her head to clear her mind. "Full blood workup, check for everything."

"You'll get a call from Cynthia on that. I'll be there in fifteen."

"Thanks, I owe you," she said.

"No problem."

JD began climbing the steps when her phone rang. "JD, it's Cynthia Phillips. Johnathan asked me to call you."

"Good to hear from you. Are you on your way?" JD walked under a shade tree as the pair spoke.

"I'm right behind you." JD turned to see her climbing the stairs and disconnected the call. "I was in the neighborhood when Johnathan called."

JD explained the situation as the two headed into the station.

Mac stood outside the conference room. "I should've known the troops would be landing. Hello, Cynthia. How are things at Phillips Pharmaceuticals?" he said, offering his hand.

Cynthia shook his hand. "Just peachy, Mac. How are things here at the great hall of injustice?" she asked, returning his firm handshake.

"Oh, wonderful, now that you two are here." No one missed his deep breath and sarcasm.

"We're always happy to be of service to the fine men in blue," JD said with a wink.

The three walked into the conference room. Derrick and Maggie, the young police technician, sat at the table.

JD suppressed a laugh as the color drained from Maggie's face at the sight of Cynthia.

"Mac, for the record, Mr. August is voluntarily, in the spirit of cooperation, providing blood, fingerprints, and DNA. No warrant necessary."

"Whatever, the warrant will be here soon," Mac said and leaned against the wall and crossed his arms and ankles.

"I gather you'd like to wait, continue to deny my client his rights?"

"Maggie, please collect the evidence," Mac half barked at the young woman.

"Yes, sir," Maggie replied in a whimper.

JD knew exactly why Maggie was intimidated. She'd ripped the girl to shreds under cross-examination last month. As a follow-up, Cynthia had reduced the technician's findings to tainted, useless evidence. Most had been beginner mistakes; JD had exploited each in her closing argument, and the client walked. Maggie hadn't built her tough skin yet. JD's eyes quickly met Cynthia's as the technician tried twice to find a vein and failed.

"Mac, are you going to torture my client or draw his blood?" JD asked.

"What do you want me to do? She's the tech on call," Mac said with a shrug.

"I'd be happy to help, if it's okay?" Cynthia offered,

her voice sweet as honey.

Mac let out a sigh and stared at Maggie. "Fine, let's get this done. This won't come back to bite me in the ass, right?" he asked, looking from Cynthia to JD.

"We both give you our word," JD answered, crossing her heart with her fingertip.

"Why doesn't that make me feel any better?"

"Maggie, remove your tourniquet," Cynthia said, then turned her attention to Derrick. "Would you like to take a minute before we continue?"

"No. Keep her away from me," Derrick said and nodded toward Maggie.

"She'll have to be part of the process, but I can minimize the pain," Cynthia said.

JD noted Maggie wincing at the statement.

Derrick stared straight ahead as Cynthia opened her bag, removed a tourniquet, placed it around his other arm, and handed him a rubber ball. "Squeeze this several times."

"Okay," Derrick said.

Cynthia traced veins with her index finger. "This will be quick and easy." She slipped on blue latex gloves, opened an alcohol swab, and disinfected his arm.

"We'll give that a few seconds to dry," Cynthia said as she secured a needle into a vacuum container. "Okay, take a deep breath and relax," she said and slipped the needle tip gently into the vein and slid a tube into place. As the blood began to flow, she released the tourniquet and took the ball from his hand.

"Maggie, after you've collected your samples, please leave the needle in place. I'll draw mine. That way, we can avoid as much discomfort as possible."

"Thank you," Maggie said and filled three red top

tubes. "I'm finished," she announced a bit too loud.

JD tracked Mac as he exited the room. Wildere Phore—the state prosecutor's presence spoke volumes. This was already on track to be a high-profile case. Ms. Phore handed Mac two documents. JD knew one was the warrant for DNA and the other was for Derrick's arrest. Through the glass, she locked eyes with Wildere. Neither could read each other's expression. They both made great poker players. JD returned her attention to the collection of evidence.

Cynthia drew three red, one each of purple, and light blue top tubes. "Just one more Derrick," she said, slipping a royal-blue-topped vacuum tube in place. As she finished, Mac entered the room. "Mac, is it all right for me to remove the needle, or does the technician need to?"

"You can," he said.

Cynthia removed it and placed folded gauze over the puncture site. "Press down firmly." She reached into her cold case and pulled out a bottle of orange juice. "Drink all of this," she said, replacing the gauze with a Band-Aid.

"JD, I have an arrest warrant for your client," Mac said, handing her the documents and stepping to Derrick.

She unfolded the sheet, fear and anger knotted inside her. She stared as the scene played out in slow motion. The words on the page were a jumble of letters. Nothing made sense.

"Let me see the warrant," Johnathan said, placing his left hand on the small of JD's back.

When had he come in? JD's hands shook as he took the papers. She'd known the arrest was coming, but she hadn't been prepared for the dizziness, panic, and the need to scream.

****

Johnathan spoke to Cynthia, "Take JD outside."

"Let's go," Cynthia said, taking JD's arm and forcing her toward the door.

Johnathan turned his attention to the prosecutor. "Wildere, I'd like to speak with my client."

"Once he's booked, he's all yours."

Johnathan dropped the warrants on the table. "Professional courtesy, five minutes."

"Mac, give them the room," the prosecutor said and exited.

"Thanks," Johnathan said, closing the door. He sat facing his friend and exploded his question. "What the hell happened?"

"I met a girl online. We made a date to, you know, play." Derrick's gaze was defiant.

"What about JD?" Johnathan asked.

"This has nothing to do with her." His jaw thrust forward.

Johnathan was irked by his cool, aloof manner. "No, you idiot. Does she take part in the lifestyle?"

"Never." He slammed his fists on the table and stood.

Johnathan looked up at the detective outside and held up his palm. "Sit down before they haul you out of here. We'll table that topic. What the hell happened?"

"We got to know each other and decided to continue the game. We drank wine, ate some cheese and crackers. The last thing I remember is tying Megan to the bed. I woke up to someone banging on the door. I was holding a knife and was covered in blood. Apparently, twelve hours had passed."

Johnathan listened to the events Derrick could recall, and drew in a deep breath. "I know you've always enjoyed alternative sex. I figured you'd given that up when JD moved in or at least when you proposed."

"I tried," Derrick said, running his hand through his hair.

"What's with the bandage on your hand?"

"There were two cuts. I'm not sure how it happened."

Johnathan leaned in. "Exactly how did you meet this woman?"

"We communicated through a website. I met her at the hotel bar, then we went to the cabin."

"What website?"

"Altlifestyle.net."

"I need your username and password," Johnathan said, removing a small notebook and pen from his jacket pocket.

Derrick didn't respond.

"I need to get in front of this. I'll shield JD as much as I can. But everything, and I mean everything, will come out in the court, not to mention the media. Every woman you've been with will be anxious to sell their story. You're a multi-millionaire. Everything you do makes the news. Until now, it has been mostly good, but the shit is about to hit the fan."

Derrick supplied the information and asked, "How long before I'll be out of here?"

"They've charged you with first-degree murder. I'll do what I can, but don't count on bail."

"But I didn't kill her. I'm being set up," Derrick blurted.

Johnathan read panic on his friend's face. "We'll get

into that later. Anything else they might find at the cabin, your home, or office?"

"Holy shit, my box." He lowered his head to the table.

"What box?" Johnathan asked and sat in silence until Derrick's eyes met his.

"It contains handcuffs, clamps, leather restraints, and sex toys."

Johnathan shook his head and continued to make notes on his pad. "We'll deal with that later. The police have it by now. You sure JD isn't into this?"

"Oh, hell no, I couldn't hurt her like that. Please take care of her. She wasn't ever supposed to know about this."

"Time's up, Counselor," Mac said, entering the room. "James Derrick August, , you are under arrest for the first-degree murder of Megan Louise Ferguson."

Johnathan was relieved Mac had interrupted their conversation. The anger toward his friend had reached a boiling point. He listened as Derrick was read his rights and placed in cuffs. "I'll take care of JD." *A whole lot better than you ever did*, he thought as one of his oldest friends was led to booking.

Chapter Three

Sleep evaded JD; she tossed and turned all night. A bit after five, she dressed and went for a run, hoping to clear her head. Instead, after three miles, she was more confused than ever and had a hundred more questions. It was time to talk to Derrick.

As an attorney, she quickly passed through security. With her professional demeanor barely intact, JD strolled into the small room for clients and attorneys.

"Good morning, Mr. August," JD said as the guard exited the room.

"Good morning, sweetheart. It's good to see you," Derrick said as he reached as far across the table as the handcuffs allowed.

JD slid her hand back. "We can't touch. Rules are the rules, even between attorney and client." That was a good excuse. JD wasn't sure she wanted him to touch her. "Derrick, we need to talk about the whole situation," she said, looking down and rubbing her forehead with her index finger.

"You're getting a migraine, aren't you?"

JD sighed and stared at Derrick. "I'll be fine."

"I've told you the truth about what happened." A muscle clenched along his jaw.

"It is not *that* night I want to discuss. I thought you were different from the others who had lied and used me. I thought you loved me, and we were happy." Tears caressed her cheeks.

Derrick stared at the hook holding his handcuffs in place. "I do love you," he whispered.

She took a deep breath, tried to force away the tension from between her shoulders, and ignored the burning in her stomach. "I feel stupid. I believed all your lies. How could I've been so wrong about you? About us? I thought we were the real thing. What was our relationship? A joke? A façade for your real life?" she said, twisting the diamond around her finger.

His fingertips touched hers. She wanted to pull away but couldn't find the strength.

"I do love you. I've never lied about that. You're the woman I want to spend the rest of my life with. The other is different."

She yanked her hands back and laughed. "Please explain? You planned to have sex with Megan. That pretty much spells it out for me." JD locked eyes with Derrick and fought to lower her voice. "Was she the only one? Don't insult me by lying. Have the balls to tell me the truth for once."

"I've never lied to you about anything that really mattered. I love you. I wanted us to grow old together." His steel-blue eyes were like cold waves when they met hers. But there was something else, a sadness she'd never seen.

She was caught off guard by the sudden vibrance in her voice. "Okay, cut the crap, Derrick." She slid her chair back, stood, and began to pace. "Explain what's different about having sex with another woman and making love to me?"

He tried to raise his hand, but the handcuffs hooked to the ring on the table stopped his motion. He glared down before continuing. "There's a part of my life I can control for a while. I was faithful until about two years ago. I fought the urges as long as I could. There are sexual things I can't do with you. The other women were merely sexual gratification." He spread his hands in frustration.

JD stopped, turned, and placed her hands on her hips. "Well, that certainly clears things up. It's nothing important, just sex. I thought I was special; how silly of me." She didn't hide the cold hurt in her statement.

"When we're together, it's making love, but it's vanilla. There're times I'm driven to do more."

She lifted her chin, meeting his icy stare straight on. "Derrick, what the hell are you talking about? Vanilla? What's vanilla?" Her shock deepened when she noticed her hands were shaking. She sat before her legs crumbled.

His fingertips touched hers. "Vanilla sex is what society regards as standard or conventional sexual practices. When we're together, it's special, sweet, and passionate. You have no idea how I love being with you. Holding. Cuddling. There's an unbelievable pleasure in satisfying you. There're no words to express the sensations I feel when we make love."

Tears clouded her eyes. "I'm really trying to understand. What is it you need that I can't give? You didn't ask me to try? We've certainly gone way beyond the missionary position."

"The things I do with other women, I can't degrade you like that." He shifted uncomfortably in the seat.

"How many other women have there been, Derrick?" JD asked, not really wanting to know but needing to hear the answer.

"Eight or ten, I think," Derrick answered, hanging his head.

JD stiffened as if Derrick had hit her. "I hope you used a condom, or didn't you think about giving me AIDS or an STD?"

"We didn't always have sex, but if we did, I wore a condom."

How could she believe him? He was apparently a champion liar. Did she really know this man at all? She shook the thoughts away. "To prepare a defense, I need to know everything. It'll come out in court anyway. You'll have to answer my questions and those of your defense team. Not to mention stories are already showing up." Triumph flooded through her when he winced at her words.

Derrick took a deep breath and slowly exhaled. "Let me try to explain. It's sadism and masochism. The practices include bondage, discipline, dominance, and submission. I enjoy being the master, spanking, tying women up, and role-playing."

"Great, I should feel better that you enjoy hurting women. I guess I should be glad you never asked me to play. If that's what you call it," JD responded in a low, angry tone. Her reactions switched with each breath.

"I never took advantage of anyone; it wasn't rape. Everything is between consenting adults." Derrick's nostrils flared as he spoke. Then he added almost as an afterthought, "My approach to sex is if the lawn is mowed at home, then it shouldn't matter how many other lawns I mow."

JD shot Derrick a glaring look before she responded. "Well, that makes everything okay. I guess I should be happy you and Paul, our lawn guy, don't share your philosophy." She shook her head and laughed. "Do you really think I'd buy this load of crap, or more importantly, the jury? They are going to think you're a sexual sadist who took the game to the next level. The ultimate high: you killed that woman." Her heart was pounding, and heat flushed through her body.

His eyes, like his words, were flat, hard, and passionless. "I didn't murder her. What I've told you is the truth. I was drugged and set up."

"We'll see what the results of the blood tests show, but that'll take weeks. I'm sure the CSI team collected a litany of evidence at the cabin. We can only wait on forensics."

"I know it looks bad, but, baby, you have to believe me," Derrick said, stretching his fingers toward hers.

JD didn't move and pretended she hadn't heard him. "That's not your only problem. There're multiple holes in your story. I'm not sure where to begin building a defense. You told Johnathan you picked her up in the hotel bar. I'm sure there'll be video evidence to support that. Our investigator checked, and she had a room at the hotel. Why, if she was planning on staying with you?"

"In case we didn't hit it off. It was the first time we met, part of the game. I didn't kill her," he said with an easy defiance.

"You're a defense attorney's nightmare. I'm more confused than ever about us and your life choices," JD answered and stood.

"You believe me, right, sweetheart?"

She read the hopeful look in his eyes. "I'm not sure about anything." JD picked up her briefcase and left the room, fighting the growing migraine. She had to escape. Her life had changed again in twenty-four hours. As quickly as the fairy tale began, it lay in ashes at her feet. What the hell was she supposed to do now?

****

JD understood there would be a search of the house she and Derrick shared, but it didn't take the sting or embarrassment out of it. Johnathan had received a heads-up from an unnamed friend, and JD thought she was mentally prepared. But at this point, with the detectives and at least fifteen members of a forensic team scouring her home, she was barely hanging on to her sanity.

It was one more event for the circus of journalists and vultures all but living on her lawn. Each one hoping to catch a picture of the wronged woman or the sexy mistress, depending on the story of the day.

Johnathan arranged a security service to guard the house, after reporters had trampled her herb garden when they scaled the stone wall in an attempt to reach the house. The five-man force kept the newshounds and groupies at bay. Her trash cans had been moved inside to avoid pilfering. She seldom went anywhere alone.

"Here, drink this," Mitch said, handing her a teacup.

"I'm not thirsty."

"Sit and drink," he said and led her to the sofa.

JD let out a long sigh. "Okay, for you." She took a gulp. The Irish whiskey-laced tea took her breath away. "Holy crap," she said after a cough.

Mitch patted her back, shrugged his shoulders, and winked.

Think about anything else, JD repeated mentally. She looked around the room and focused on Benjamin Cheatem. His dark-red hair and close-cropped beard, combined with the deep-green eyes, left no doubt he was Irish long before the brogue gave his ancestry away.

Unlike Johnathan, Benjamin avoided the limelight of the courtroom; he preferred contracts. Finding ways to break the unbreakable or create airtight agreements. Benjamin taught JD to pick the law apart and analyze it. *"Sit back and listen when the world seems out of control, in chaos,"* he'd told her, *"there's profit. It might as well help their clients."* That certainly applied today.

Johnathan's touch brought JD back to the room. He sat on the sofa beside her as Mac approached.

Mac stood over JD, staring down. "I should've known the whole gang would be here," he said, making eye contact with the four before turning his focus to JD. "Do you know where Mr. August's computers are?"

"Mac, sit down; staring up makes my neck hurt," JD said, motioning to the chair. When he didn't move, she added, "I'll answer your questions. Please sit down."

"If you gentlemen are hungry, I've set up snacks and lemonade in the dining room," JD heard Mitch announce.

"Mitch, the officers don't have time to stop and eat," Mac said, running his hand through his hair. "Would you let my men do their jobs?"

"Sorry, Mac, this is the first time I've been at a house-search party. I wasn't sure what to serve," Mitch said as he traipsed to a wingback chair, sat, and crossed his legs. Mitch's dark shoulder-length hair was pulled into a ponytail. His handlebar mustache suited his quirky bow tie and outrageous seasonal jacket. It all combined to add another absurd angle to this shit show.

JD knew, in retrospect, the situation would be funny, but right now, not so much. It did take the edge off a bit that Mac seemed to have lost control of the situation, if only for an instant. "Okay, Mac, what do you want to know?" JD asked, wringing her hands.

"Do you know how many computers Mr. August owns?"

"Three, I think." *But what did she know, really?* She counted on her fingers as she tried to concentrate. "The desktop here, one of the same at his office, and a small one he carries everywhere."

"Do you know where his laptop and phone are?"

"No." JD continued to glance at the officers moving around her home.

"Is there a safe in the house?"

"Yes, we have two. One for my jewelry, the other a gun safe. I'm happy to open them or give you the codes."

"Would you open them?"

"You want me to do that now?" JD asked, rising.

"Yes."

JD held tight to her fragile control as she headed to her walk-in closet, opened the floor-to-ceiling mirror, and entered the ten-digit code. She opened the door and stepped back. "The gun safe is in Derrick's office." She slipped her hands into her jeans pockets.

"Would you open that one? Please," he added as an afterthought.

JD took a deep breath as she walked across the hallway. She felt a punch to her gut as she paused momentarily at Derrick's office door. *What a master manipulator he was, and she'd fallen for it all, hook, line, and sinker.* She opened the double doors and repeated the process. "I know your team is being respectful with their search. Thanks for that."

Before he could respond, an officer interrupted, "There's another safe in this closet."

Surprised, she stared tongue-tied at the officer. Her

cheeks burned in embarrassment.

"JD, did you know about the safe?"

"No," she said, moving her head left to right. Tears stung in the back of her eyes; she battled not to cry. "Maybe it's the same code as the gun safe. You want me to try to open it?" *More secrets coming out.*

"Yes."

JD's hands trembled as she tried the code three times. "I guess this is one more thing he lied about." She turned, and Johnathan folded her into his arms and held tight as she sobbed.

"Mac, I'm going to take her downstairs," Johnathan said over JD's head.

The search continued for hours. JD sat on the sofa between Mitch and Benjamin. Johnathan ran interference as needed. When the officers left, JD surveyed the damage.

Mitch squatted in front of JD and took her hands. "Girlfriend, you're coming home with me. You're all coming with me," he said, looking around the room. "We'll tackle this later."

JD began to protest, but the words died in her throat. She followed Mitch to the car, slipped into the front seat, and let her head drop into her hands. Her world was a carnival sideshow. Nothing was as it appeared. Had Derrick's friends really come to her rescue? Or did they have secrets, like Derrick? Did she know them as well as she thought? Were they into the lifestyle too? Could all or one of them have set this up? Her head and neck throbbed. She wanted to go to sleep and never wake up.

JD rummaged through her purse, found the medicine bottle, and rattled it. Perhaps this is the answer; she could take the pills and be free. Escape the pain, the betrayal, the guilt, everything. Why was she never good enough? Why couldn't she live a normal life? She rested her head against the seat back and considered the options. Perhaps it was time to let go; the pills would be quick and painless. Who would really care? She'd simply be a headline in tomorrow's paper. Tears rained down JD's cheeks as despair swallowed her whole.

Chapter Four

"Good morning," Johnathan said as the guard handcuffed Derrick to the table.

"Is JD still in security?" Derrick asked as he looked around Johnathan toward the door.

"She's not with me. You need to answer some tough questions, not crafted responses for her benefit. Plus, the police searched your house yesterday. JD was blindsided when they found the second safe in your office. She went home with Mitch. He's holding her hostage today." Johnathan removed a pad from his briefcase and a pen from his jacket pocket.

"Would you ask her to come see me tomorrow? I need to see her; it's one of the few good things I have to hold on to."

Selfish jackass, thinking only of himself, as usual. Johnathan pushed the anger down. JD deserved much more, but he couldn't be part of the puzzle now. "Sure, I'll ask."

"Okay. Did they find anything in my safe?"

"Not that I saw."

Derrick let out a long, slow breath and grinned. "That's good. There's a secret compartment. Mitch knows about it. I'll have him clean it out."

"Do I want to know what that's about?"

"Probably not."

"Okay." Johnathan filed the information away and

continued, "Where are your phone and laptop?"

"Like I said before, at the cabin."

"Not according to the police evidence list. Did you hide them?"

"No. They were on the dresser. I was going to video—" Derrick hung his head.

Johnathan looked at the ceiling. "Okay, when the laptop surfaces, which it will, it's safe to say we're going to have problems. One of the officers probably lifted it. They'll wait until the trial or sell the information." He forced a controlled tone. "What's on it?"

"Business files, emails, my diary, pictures and videos of women. None of it will be good for my defense. One upside is the information is highly encrypted. Three tries and the data's toast," Derrick said, laying his hands open.

"Anything backed up any place?"

"Nope."

"Okay, did Megan have a phone or laptop?"

"Yep, both."

"Those are missing as well, but I'm sure they'll turn up too." Johnathan jotted notes on his pad. "We'll wait and see. Nothing else we can do. Tell me again about the night Megan died."

"We met at the hotel bar, went back to the cabin, drank wine, got to know each other, discussed the ground rules—you know how the game is played."

"It's been a long time. What happened next?" Johnathan asked without looking up.

Derrick shifted in his chair. "Like I keep saying over and over. After we decided to move forward, I tied her to the bed and lay beside her. Megan said she wasn't feeling well. That's the last thing I remember. That's why I think we were drugged. There had to be something in the wine."

"Nothing showed up in our blood work; some tests are still pending. The wine bottle and glasses came back negative for any substance other than wine, and for the hat trick, the only fingerprints were yours and Megan's. The wounds are consistent with the attacker lying beside her. Before you ask, I have a friend at the police department who slipped me information. It'll come out during discovery, but anything we get early helps."

"I'm being set up; that's the only answer," Derrick said, shaking his head.

"Okay, by who?"

"I don't know. I've been racking my brain trying to figure it out. I've made enemies along the way, but it must be someone close to set me up this tight."

"The police are covering all the bases. I'm sure JD will be questioned soon."

"JD, seriously?" Derrick's loud laughter filled the room. "She's smart, but not this smart. Plus, she had no idea what was going on."

Johnathan clenched his teeth and pressed his lips together, harnessing the anger, and decided to let the subject drop. "Is there anyone from your business dealings or the BDSM community who'd have a grudge and enough knowledge to do this? Anyone obsessed with you?"

Derrick picked at his fingernails as he thought. "There was one couple, Lois and Ron Mitchell. We got together a few times, then I started getting a strange vibe. I cut ties. They continued to contact me. I made excuses, and the messages stopped."

"Did they ever go to the cabin?"

"No."

"Who did?"

Johnathan made notes as Derrick named three people. "I read your communications on altlifestyle.net and didn't find anyone that stuck out to investigate. The only facts we have pointing to a third party are the missing computers and phones, but that can be explained. You disposed of them after you killed Megan."

"I didn't kill her."

Johnathan leaned in, locked eyes with Derrick, and lowered his voice. "I need to ask you something, and think before you answer. Did you kill Megan?" Derrick started to speak, but Johnathan held up his hand. "In college, you were playing, and a girl died. We took your word it was a reaction to the meth, and never discussed it again."

He watched the color drain from his friend's face. "I need to know what happened with Megan. If it was an accident or—" He stopped when Derrick held up his hand.

"What happened at university wasn't my fault, and I still don't want to talk about it. I've told you everything about the night with Megan. My memory stops."

Memory loss again, that's convenient. "It doesn't look good. The firm's investigators keep coming up empty. The prosecutor's hinting at a possible plea deal to take the death penalty off the table. You interested?"

"No! Dammit, I'm not. I didn't kill her. I'm paying you a great deal of money to handle my defense. Something will turn up; I know it. I can't spend the rest of my life in here for something I didn't do." Derrick raised his fists the few inches he could and slammed them on the metal table.

"Okay, okay," Johnathan said, holding up his hands. "As your attorney, I have to let you know about communications with the prosecutor. We'll keep working every angle. Anything you need?"

"To see JD. How is she doing?"

"Putting on a brave front. Benjamin, Mitch, and I are doing everything we can to shield her, but her world has been turned upside down, and the press is relentless. She's questioning everything, including who you are and what she really was to you. I'm concerned about her physical and mental health. I tried to get her to slow down, but you know how she is."

"Like a dog with a bone," Derrick said.

"I'm your attorney but also your friend. As so, you need to make sure JD is okay. Not for now, but what happens after the trial, either way it goes. You understand? You need to make this situation right. If you are acquitted, do you really think you can pick up where things were?"

"I know it's different, but JD loves me, and things will be okay. I'll find a way around her objections; we'll get married and move on."

Johnathan wanted to laugh; this arrogant SOB believed he couldn't be convicted. Derrick was a master manipulator who'd always gotten his way. In all the years they'd been friends, Johnathan couldn't remember anyone saying no to Derrick. Well, anyone who wasn't convinced, one way or the other, to change their mind.

****

JD rubbed sweaty palms on her slacks. It wasn't the first time she'd been in a police interrogation room, but this was different. She was here for questioning, not as an attorney reassuring a client. She was nervous and had to admit the surroundings were intimidating.

She was developing a healthy, new respect for those she represented. It was a learning experience being on the other side of the game. Since Derrick's arrest, she'd known, as his fiancée, she'd be considered a suspect. One more thing added to the rollercoaster of emotions assaulting her mind and body.

At least she'd been smart enough to bring an attorney—like she'd had a choice. Benjamin and Johnathan had almost come to blows over who would represent her.

****

JD allowed her mind to drift back to the encounter, anything to calm her racing thoughts. She'd been staring at the same page of a law journal when Benjamin and Johnathan entered her office. She hadn't read a word in hours. Her mind was reeling from the events since Derrick's incarceration.

She slid her glasses atop her head and looked up. The pair approached like two tomcats protecting their turf.

JD fought to suppress her laugh. They looked so serious. "What's up? You two look like you're ready to square off for a duel."

Benjamin spoke first. "I heard through the grapevine Detective MacWilliams wants to question you."

"Routine stuff, we're sure," Johnathan reassured her.

"I know. I spoke with him earlier. Told him I'd be in tomorrow at ten," JD said, closing the book and walking around her desk.

"You didn't think to share that little tidbit with us?"

Johnathan asked.

"I'll clear my calendar and go with you," Benjamin said before JD could respond.

"I'll go with her. I'm the defense litigator," Johnathan said, walking within inches of Benjamin.

"We'll both go," Benjamin argued, puffing out his chest.

JD rolled her eyes and stepped between the two. "That's all I need. Nothing says I've nothing to hide like two senior partners from what is arguably one of the most prestigious law firms in the United States flanking their client in for routine questioning."

In the end, the two men had flipped a coin.

Johnathan seemed too proud of himself, slipping the quarter back into his pocket. "You want to do lunch?" he asked.

"I'm a bit busy," she said, glancing at her desk. "With all the male testosterone in the room, I think you two should go do something manly. I know; go to the shooting range."

"Nope, lunch it is," Johnathan said, motioning with his hand toward the door.

Benjamin added, "Since you won the coin toss, you get to buy lunch. I think Mitch has a steak with my name on it."

"Okay, sore loser," Johnathan said.

Somehow, they always seemed to know when she needed them. She shrugged and said, "How could I refuse?" After a short pause, she added, "Especially if I want to make partner." She teased and faked a smile.

"Smart lady," Johnathan said, lifting her jacket from the black, wrought iron dachshund coatrack.

"We going to make her a partner?" Benjamin asked

Johnathan with a chuckle. Amusement flickered in the eyes that met hers.

JD slipped into her navy jacket.

"When she grows up," Johnathan responded.

JD replied, "Well, I can always call—"

Benjamin interrupted her mid-sentence by holding up his finger. "Don't even say it, or it's back to the Wills and Trusts Department with you."

"She did do a good job down there," Johnathan bantered with a laugh.

"I thought you were taking me to lunch?" JD said.

****

Mentally, back in the interview room, JD thought she'd always work at the firm of Dewey, Cheatam, and Howe. Her heart skipped a beat—unless they thought the chaos with Derrick would damage the firm's reputation. She closed her eyes and blew out a deep breath, trying to force away the cloud of trepidation building inside her.

Johnathan and Benjamin might overlook the damage since Derrick had been a friend since college and was a paying client. But Mr. Cheatam, the firm's final founding partner's grandson, was another story. Anger at Derrick surged through her; he'd lied, cheated, and now would take the one thing she knew was real, and she'd achieved herself.

JD was ripped back to reality by voices. She bit her bottom lip, her fingers clenched in her lap.

"Hello, JD, Johnathan. Thanks for coming in," Detective MacWilliams said as he took a seat and placed a recorder on the table. Turning it on, he said, "Just routine."

"No problem," JD said.

"Would you mind stating your name for the

record?"

"Jennifer Dianne Ellis."

"I asked you to come in to discuss the murder of Megan Ferguson."

"Okay," JD said, shrugging her shoulders.

"What's your relationship to Derrick August?"

So, the cat and mouse would begin. "We're engaged," she answered, holding up her left hand and flashing the ring.

"How would you characterize your relationship with Mr. August?"

"I thought it was good, excellent, actually," JD said, pushing down the sudden wave of nausea. *What an idiot I'd been.*

"Did you know Mr. August was involved with other women? Did you participate in the alternative sexual lifestyle?"

"No," JD said, fighting back the tears as emotions tore through her already-achy body.

"Did you have knowledge of Mr. August's other sexual activities?" Mac leaned in as he asked.

JD shook her head.

Johnathan touched JD on the shoulder. "My client has no knowledge related to this line of questioning; next topic, Mac."

"Where were you on Friday night, February 16, 2000?"

JD's eyes met the detective's. "I was home," she answered and folded her sweating palms in her lap.

"What time did you arrive home?"

She paused briefly to collect her thoughts. "I had a migraine and left work early, about three, I think," she said, turning to Johnathan. "I'm sure HR can pull a copy of my time sheet."

"Was anyone with you?" Mac asked.

"No. I was alone. The headache was one of the worst I've had. I took my strongest medication and went to bed," JD said, willing her clenched fingers to relax.

"Do you have migraines often?"

"Yes. They're connected to my menstrual cycle. Over the last year, I've missed several hours each month from work. The medication is almost as debilitating as the headaches."

"So, you don't have an alibi for the night of the murder," Detective MacWilliams stated and sat back in his chair.

Johnathan met Mac's gaze and opened a manila folder. "We have paperwork that might help establish my client's alibi." Johnathan continued his dialogue as he handed each document to the detective. "A statement from her physician outlining her treatment and the side effects of the medication. Phone company records showing my client's phone never left her residence. And finally, a statement from the security company providing no alarms were triggered to indicate anyone exited the residence from three thirty p.m. when Ms. Ellis arrived home until the next morning."

"Guess it's your client's good fortune she has state-of-the-art home security." His voice was low and smooth as he scanned the documents.

"I've been a defense attorney for a long time and simply anticipated what you'd need. Is there any other information we can provide?" Johnathan asked.

JD bit back the chuckle and hoped her smile was noncommittal. Johnathan had never lost a case the TPD brought against one of his clients. She thought he was enjoying the banter a bit too much.

"Do you know where Mr. August's laptop and phone are?" Mac asked, still studying the paperwork.

"No," JD said, straightening in the chair.

"Do you have any other questions?" Johnathan asked.

"Not at this time. JD, thanks for coming in. I may need to speak with you again."

"We're only a phone call away," Johnathan said, standing and sliding JD's chair back.

Alone in the elevator, JD turned to Johnathan and laughed. "You enjoyed that way too much."

He shrugged and replied, "You know it's all part of the game. I'm sure he'll want to question you again."

"At least I haven't been named a person of interest," JD said, forcing a smile.

"That may change, at least in the press, when word gets out you were called in for questioning," Johnathan said, exiting the elevator and steering JD toward the main entrance.

JD slipped on her sunglasses. Johnathan opened the door, and they were met by a barrage of reporters. "I think the cat is out of the bag," she whispered.

Johnathan slid his arm around her waist and led her to a car waiting at the curb. He only spoke once to the many questions yelled as they passed. "We have no comment at this time."

JD recognized the driver as the office runner. "Thanks, Frank. How did you know we needed a rescue?"

"Mr. Dewey wanted me around, so here I am," he said, meeting her eyes in the rearview mirror.

JD rested her head on the seat back. She closed her

eyes and fought to slow her galloping heart. So, this was her new normal. She'd learned to live in Derrick's spotlight and would handle this as well. Yes, she'd deal with whatever came next. She was a survivor and had proven that time and time again.

Chapter Five

"You can't be in court as part of the defense team." Johnathan held up his hand when JD tried to speak. "Think about it. Everyone, especially the jury, will be watching your every facial expression, action, and reaction. If they believe for one second you doubt Derrick's innocence, it's over; we're done."

Benjamin joined the ambush. "I don't want you there at all. Work behind the scenes. You're the best researcher I know." He sat beside her and patted her hand like that would reduce the insult.

JD sprang up. Her world spun out of control as she stared at the evidence board and counted to ten before she faced them. "Derrick needs me there. Hell, I need to be there. What if you miss something? I can't believe you're shutting me out." The shaky words came out in a shout. She wasn't sure who was more shocked, her or them.

She stormed from the conference room, down the hall, and into an open elevator. She hit the button so hard she was surprised it didn't shatter. She paced around the elevator, trying to find her center and breathe. *Who the hell did they think they were? Telling her what to do. Men! Men! Lying, cheating, backstabbing assholes, all of them.* JD stomped out of the elevator and charged through the glass doors into the sunshine of the roof garden.

The tightness in her throat choked her, and dizziness and nausea hit her like a strong breeze. She more fell into the chair than sat. The large diamond on her finger cast a prism across the tile floor. This wasn't what her world was supposed to be. She should be preparing for her wedding, not visiting her groom in jail. When had everything gotten so out of control? What decisions had led her to this hell?

JD dropped her face in her hands and let the tears come. She couldn't hold them back any longer. Who was she kidding? Life as she knew it was over. She'd dared to dream and overreach. Her father had said she'd fail, and she did. Hadn't she turned out like he said, a junkie crack whore like her mother? That's what she was, another whore in Derrick's stable of women. Crack was not her drug of choice—money, nice clothes, and the fancy life were.

Was she any better than the women her father had beaten and forced to work for him? Like he'd tried to do with her at age sixteen? Derrick hadn't hit her but instead used her to cover up the BDSM life he really wanted to live.

She was caught up in the downward spiral now; memories flashed back. She was back in the abandoned building, hiding after she overheard her parents discussing how much they could make selling her. How they'd watched over her to make sure she remained a virgin. People would pay big for a young, pretty, unspoiled girl. It was time their investment paid off.

She left that day, her sixteenth birthday. She'd taken money from her father's stash. Enough to survive, but not enough to set him off. He'd been passed out on the couch, her mother satisfying a john in the bedroom when she slipped away with only the things that fit in a backpack.

She'd gotten on a bus to Florida and lived in shelters. She'd done about anything to survive except sell herself.

Her life changed when she met Anna Scott, a social worker at a homeless shelter. She helped JD become emancipated and get her GED. Another situation she'd trusted that went wrong. The scene of Anna dead on the sidewalk, a victim of a random shooting, played out in her mind.

Yet another wave of panic rolled over JD. She hadn't considered the possibility the scandal might get the attention of her father. He'd happily come forward to sell his version of her childhood story to the highest bidder. One more terrifying "what if" in her life.

JD beat her fists on her knees until she was sure there would be bruises. "No, no, no!" she shouted to the sky. She had to take charge, it was her life, and she wouldn't allow Derrick or anyone else to be in control. JD held her aching head in her hands. Johnathan and Benjamin were right.

Johnathan was a force to be reckoned with in and out of the courtroom. His slim athletic form moved with the grace of a ballet dancer. JD learned all she knew about courtroom theatrics, watching him pull jurors into closing arguments. He was a master storyteller, bending the facts many seasoned prosecutors thought outlined an open-and-shut case into an acquittal for his clients.

Benjamin would analyze the hell out of anything brought up at trial. He'd taught her to sit back, watch people, and listen. She took in their words and movements; they often told two different stories.

Johnathan and Benjamin were the defense team Derrick needed.

JD scrubbed her face with her hands. It was time to apologize and eat crow. She stood and adjusted her jacket as pain lanced through her chest and head, nausea swept over her, her chest constricted, she couldn't breathe, and sweat poured down her back. JD tried to focus through the ringing in her ears. Her hand shook so violently her cell crashed on the tile floor. *I'm dying* was her last thought before the world turned black and swallowed her.

****

Johnathan read the disappointment on Derrick's face as he and Benjamin entered the room.

"Good morning," both men said in tandem.

"What's up? JD not with you?" Derrick asked.

"Not today. How are you doing?" Johnathan said, pulling out a chair and taking a seat.

"As best I can," Derrick said, trying to raise his shackled wrists.

"You know we're doing everything possible. Your team's working around the clock," Benjamin said, walking to the barred window.

Derrick's response came with a forced chuckle. "Yeah, I saw the bill."

"We've been friends for a long time," Johnathan said, shifting to face his client.

"Probably more than any of us care to admit. What's up? I know when something's on your mind." Derrick directed his stare to Benjamin.

"It's JD," Benjamin said, leaning against the wall, crossing his arms.

"What? Is she okay?" Derrick said, arching forward,

panic lacing his tone.

"She was discharged from the hospital, but we have concerns," Benjamin continued.

"What happened?"

Johnathan answered this time. "Wendi found her unconscious in the rooftop garden." He left out the argument and her storming out. "The diagnosis was exhaustion. All she does is work to make her billable hours and concentrate on your case. She's lost weight, and there're always dark circles around her eyes. Have you looked, I mean, really looked at her lately?"

"I know." Derrick hung his head. "I told her to cut back."

"Benjamin and I are going to insist she take time off. Get away from the office and the barrage of media. The scandal is still front-page news. It is clear the embarrassment and humiliation are taking their toll."

"You know how JD is; she won't go," Derrick said.

"We're going to make her an offer she can't refuse," Benjamin said, placing his palms down on the steel table.

"We need to make sure you're on board and will support us," Johnathan said.

"Like many things since my arrest, it doesn't really sound like I have a choice."

"We're working every angle," Benjamin said, sitting next to his partner.

"I know." He sighed heavily, his voice filled with anguish as he continued. "I'll always do what's best for JD. Guard, I want to go back to my cell," Derrick said.

Johnathan waited until Derrick was gone before he tapped the door. As they exited the jail, neither spoke. Johnathan's thoughts were on JD, not Derrick. The lousy son of a bitch deserved whatever he got. Treating JD the way he had. What had Derrick been thinking? Another woman was dead. Had he taken the game too far?

Benjamin touched Johnathan on the shoulder. "You okay?"

Johnathan stopped and faced his friend, his voice a whisper. "Yeah. I've got a couple of theories that keep circling."

"Okay, tell me," Benjamin said.

"If someone really knew Derrick, I mean about his other life, like we do. It would be very easy to frame him. Is there anyone that comes to mind? Or could this be connected to the incident in college?" Johnathan saw the fire flash in his friend's eyes.

Benjamin stepped to Johnathan. He pointed his index finger in his companion's face, hostility surging through his tone. "That's dead and buried. We did nothing wrong. We were kids in the wrong place at the wrong time."

Johnathan's response was cold as ice. "Were we really? We only have Derrick's side of the story. We didn't push for details; we just let it go."

Benjamin turned and walked toward the car. Johnathan followed. Neither spoke for the ride back to the office.

****

JD tossed her glasses atop the ocean of crime scene photos and reports littering her desk. At least she could look at them now without throwing up, so much violence and blood. Small cuts beginning at the feet, continuing up the body, each slice deeper until the coup de grâce: the woman's throat was slit.

The coroner's report documented the location, length, and depth of each wound. The forensic technicians hadn't missed a thing. The black-and-white photographs with their alphanumeric cones and evidence markers recorded in explicit detail the slaughter of the woman tied to the bed. Blood splatter patterns and arterial spurting circled in yellow jumped from the page.

A random killing had been ruled out. No tool marks, or signs of forced entry, were found on the doors or windows. Derrick's handprint was on the headboard, in blood. No footprints except Derrick's.

JD sighed and examined the picture of the bite mark on the victim's shoulder, dropped the photo, and again reviewed the DNA report of the saliva swabbed from the wound. Positive match for Derrick, same as his blood and fingerprints on the knife. The only explanation for this was he stabbed the woman so violently that his hand slipped during the attack, and he cut himself. Even Johnathan, the best attorney she knew, was mystified by the evidence and found no other scenario to explain it.

She felt like a burst helium balloon blown to and fro without any control, now flat, deflated on the ground. All she could do was wait for another gust of wind to push her over the edge. Shoving back the chair, she stood, turned toward the window, and rolled her shoulders, trying to release the tension. The all too familiar throb at the base of her skull grew more intense. A killer migraine was looming. She closed her eyes and rubbed the bridge of her nose.

How many times had she ripped a page from her calendar since her life had imploded? Six, eight, ten, twelve? Yep, twelve. Time seemed to crawl and rush by at the same time, yet the trial was still months away. Her anguish peaked and shattered the last shreds of her control. Tears pooled in her eyes. She closed them tight and forced the calm back. The doctor had warned her; the panic attacks were a warning signal from her body. She had to relax. How the hell was she supposed to do that?

The prosecution was continuing to build their case. If she didn't find something soon, best-case scenario, Derrick would face life in prison without the possibility of parole. Worst case lethal injection. The deep sigh seemed to crawl up from her toes to escape her lips. Did he really deserve this?

She sat on the window ledge and let the sun hit her face. Derrick, her client, her fiancé, the man she loved, had admitted to it all. Well, everything but the murder. He confessed to taking part in the BDSM lifestyle most of his adult life and enjoying knife play. How had she missed this huge part of his life and for so long? How could she have been so naïve?

She caught sight of a hawk floating on the thermals and wished she could fly away. What did she really know about Derrick? One thing she knew—he was an expert liar and a fraud. The constant travel for his import-export business made perfect sense now. How could she still care? How could she still love him? Did she still love him? She needed to use the same cold detachment as she did with her clients: shut out sentiment and work the case. But how could she do that?

The firm's investigators had uncovered nothing except more incriminating evidence. The number of women he'd victimized continued to grow. Twenty in all as of yesterday. He couldn't even be truthful about that. Oh, the things she'd learned about this alternative lifestyle, unfortunately, a great deal came from the media. Pictures and the stories of Derrick's women appeared regularly in the tabloids. True or not, it was what people were still talking about.

She'd changed her phone numbers and emails several times. The firm administrator had moved her parking underground to supply protection from the onslaught of reporters. She was shut off from the world. All she had was work. At least here, she'd found a mindless solidarity that helped camouflage her deep despair of loneliness. Thank goodness she still had this refuge.

JD stood and paced; it was then she caught her reflection in the mirror. Shocked, she stepped closer, leaned in, and ran her fingers across her face. Who was the woman staring back at her? Deep, dark rings circled hollow, lifeless eyes. Taking in the whole picture caused an audible gasp. She'd lost weight. The silk blouse and suit skirt hung on her. When had this transformation taken place? Did she look this bad in the hospital? Somehow it hadn't registered then. Even her expensive makeup couldn't hide the stress and defeat.

"What does it matter?" she murmured to the clouds. Hot tears escaped down her cheeks. "What did anything matter? It was time to face facts. My life is based on lies and deceit." The words escaped her lips and rang in her head.

"JD."

She jumped at the sound of Johnathan's voice, wiped her eyes, and turned toward the doorway. Swallowing the sob that stuck in her throat, she looked up.

"Hey," she halfheartedly responded. As Benjamin and Johnathan entered her office, she fought off the growing dread. She forced the positive, happy tone before continuing, "Good afternoon, gentlemen. To what do I owe the pleasure of a visit by two senior partners?"

"We need to talk," Benjamin said and shut the door. Both men took a chair in front of her desk.

"Okay. It must be bad. You both look very serious." She let out a nervous laugh. "Is it Derrick? Is he okay?"

"Derrick's fine. I guess this is an intervention," Benjamin said, glancing to Johnathan.

"An intervention?" JD questioned.

"Let's call it that for now," Johnathan said.

His expression was grim. She leaned forward. "Okay, what's up?" *They were going to fire her. The reporters camped outside the firm, the constant calls. She should've seen it coming. What the hell would she do now?* Desolation stabbed her in the chest.

"Two things: one, we want to offer you a partnership."

"What? You announce partners in the fall." The fear and terror slipped away as quickly as it had gathered inside. "But okay."

Johnathan stroked his beard. "Do you want us to wait until fall?"

"No. I'm surprised, shocked, actually. My work of late has been, well, not as good as I know it should be. Plus, all the problems Derrick's case has brought to the firm."

"Comes with the territory. I gather you plan to accept?" Benjamin asked, letting a smile cross his lips.

"Certainly." She stood and walked around the desk.

"Good," Benjamin said, offering her his hand.

"Why does this feel like the good part of a good-news-bad-news situation?" JD asked, shaking Johnathan's hand. "Let the other shoe drop already," she continued, fighting the urge to do the happy dance.

"She never misses anything." Johnathan said, turning to Benjamin.

"Okay, spill it. One of you," she said with a half laugh—the first time in a long time, she realized.

"We want you to take some time off," Benjamin said.

"Time off?" She sat back on her desk. "How long?"

"Six or eight weeks."

"Why?" JD struggled with the uncertainty growing in her stomach.

"Can we be honest?" Johnathan said, letting out a long, slow breath.

"Of course," JD said.

Johnathan held her hand. "You're running yourself ragged. You've been through the wringer this past year. Then there's the small matter of your recent hospital stay. You've lost weight and look like. well, to be honest, like shit," he continued, placing his hands on her shoulders.

"Don't hold back. Tell me how you really feel." JD let the sarcasm shine through loud and clear.

Benjamin spoke. "There's a place in Arizona. It comes highly recommended, very discreet. No one will know where you are or why but us and Mitch." He shifted his eyes to Johnathan and back. "I made the arrangements myself. Not even the best reporters will be able to find you. We'll divide your work and keep Wendi busy. Take the time, JD."

"I'm not sure I want to," JD said, preparing the argument in her head.

Benjamin continued, "Let me make it a bit easier. If you want the partnership, you'll take the time."

When she had nothing to say, Johnathan added, "You know it's for the best. If you keep up this pace, you'll be no good for anyone, not Derrick, the firm, nor yourself."

"When you put it that way, when do I leave?" Resigned, JD raised her hands in surrender. Her emotions were on a monster roller coaster again. She might as well buckle up and enjoy the ride because she really didn't have a choice.

Chapter Six

Johnathan felt her presence before she spoke. Perhaps it was her sweet smell that stirred him.

"Hello, boss," JD said, strolling into his office.

She was tan, toned, and glowing. He knew from the discreet weekly reports she was doing great but wasn't ready for the woman who stood before him. "Wow! The time away certainly agreed with you. You look amazing." The cotton dress clung to her curves, and the heels showed off gorgeous legs. He stood, walked around his desk, and extended his hand. "It's good to have you back."

"Really, a handshake," she said and stepped in to hug him. "Thank you so much," she whispered before stepping back.

"When did you get back?" he asked, fighting to keep his libido in check.

"This morning. I wanted to come by and say thanks. Since I'm barred from working until Monday, I'm going to spend the weekend riding my bike and getting settled. Unless you have some work for me now?" she asked with a smile.

"Nope, deal's a deal. Do you have time for lunch? I'll catch you up. Benjamin and I are scheduled to go in about thirty minutes."

"Lunch sounds great; I'm starving."

"Good. You've taken up biking?" Johnathan asked,

returning to his chair.

"Yep. About twenty miles three days a week. My new obsession," she said, shrugging her shoulders.

"Perhaps we can ride sometime?" Johnathan forced his eyes to stay on hers and not take a slow journey down her body.

"I'd love to. I'll check in with Wendi. Be back in thirty."

Johnathan watched her almost bounce out of his office. Damn, the woman was amazing. In her absence, he'd realized how often he went out of his way to pass her office.

He'd been drawn to her from the moment they'd met. Derrick had bragged about a new girlfriend for weeks and finally brought JD to a BBQ at Mitch's farm. They saw each other briefly at events but never really talked. He was sure she was another in Derrick's parade of ladies.

When Derrick asked him to interview JD for a summer clerk position, he'd agreed out of friendship, but when she entered the room dressed to impress, he felt like a tongue-tied schoolboy. By the end of the interview, he discovered she was wicked smart, and her knowledge of the law was well ahead of any intern he'd hired before.

Johnathan's lips curved in a smile. He wasn't sure they'd actually hired her after graduation; it was a given she'd stay. JD used the negotiation skills learned from Benjamin to secure a great salary-and-benefits package. The investment had paid off in spades. She brought in new clients and was now one of the firm's best litigators.

As a partner, she needed a new office. In her absence, a storage room and small conference area were converted into a suite. Coastal pastels and gray furniture suited her style and personality. The south-facing windows overlooked the picturesque Tallahassee capital skyline.

The only downside of her partnership, leave of absence, and office renovation was it had the law firm gossip mill working overtime. There was nothing he could do about it, nor did he really care.

He rose and took in the view from his office window. A gust of wind blew orange and yellow leaves from the hundred-year-old oak trees, forming a blanket in the small park below. Black, billowy clouds were moving in, bringing with them a storm, much like his internal war raging over his feelings for JD.

Guilt shifted his thoughts to Derrick. He was going to be convicted unless investigators could pull a miracle out of their asses. His old friend would probably spend the next fifteen to twenty years on death row. Was he guilty? All the evidence pointed there, or did it, really?

The pieces fit together. That was the problem. It was too neatly packaged, complete with a big red bow. There had to be a thread he could find, pull, and unravel the mystery.

He knew many things from Derrick's past. In college, he'd had a secret benefactor and would never tell who she was. Following graduation, Derrick seemed to be rolling in money. Again, he hadn't explained. Mitch had seen the women supporting Derrick, or so he said. The two had connected at once the day they met. Maybe there was something there. He made a note to ask both men about the mysterious woman and what happened to her.

Deep down, he felt there was a part of the puzzle missing. He couldn't put his finger on it. What would happen between him and JD if Derrick was found guilty? What was wrong with him? They'd been friends for years, and here he was lusting after Derrick's girlfriend, but hadn't he been for years? Johnathan let out a deep sigh and returned to his desk.

****

JD hung her sweater on the metal chair and paced the small room. Her stomach was turning flip-flops. She hadn't seen Derrick since her trip to Arizona. As he entered, she was glad there was a table between them.

"Look at you, wow, what a transformation," he said as the guard cuffed him to the bar on the table.

JD sat. "Thank you. I've been biking. Nothing in my closet fits. I've had to buy new clothes. I made partner," JD said all in one breath. Derrick looked worse than when she'd left. He'd lost weight, and his eyes were dull and lifeless.

"Sweetie, that's wonderful. I told you you'd make partner. I wish I could hug you," Derrick said.

"You were always my biggest supporter, believed in me when I doubted myself. I'm ready to take a fresh look at your case. I hadn't been to the mall in ages. I took Wendi with me. To say the least, we got carried away. I don't think I've ever had this many new things, except when you first took me shopping." A tinge of guilt danced across her mind recalling the shopping bags and clothes cluttering the spare bedrooms. Not one outfit placed in a special cloth bag.

Derrick made her nervous. Something right under the surface was different, almost like he wasn't pleased with the transformation. JD realized she was babbling.

"I'm glad you're doing better; I was worried about you. There's something we need to discuss."

"Okay."

"I want you to sell the house on Lake Ella." The look on his face devastated her. She knew how much he loved the property.

"Why?"

Derrick let out a long audible sigh and momentarily looked at his hands cuffed to the table. "Baby, when this is over, we'll need a fresh start. You can buy a new place or move into one of the rental properties."

"Is that really what you want?" JD shifted in her chair.

"Put it on the market. Meet with Mitch. We have multiple joint ventures. Promise me you'll do what I ask with the money."

"Okay," JD said as the old, familiar panic began to creep in.

"Use some of the money to pay off our rental properties, and put the rest in your account. Mitch will handle my legal fees and make a monthly deposit into your account. If you need more, go to Mitch. You'll never want for anything no matter what happens."

"Why all this now?"

"It doesn't matter; just listen. Draw up the paperwork to remove my name from the rental property deeds. That will give you another source of income. This is my problem, not yours. Promise me." His stern eyes locked with hers.

"Okay, I promise." JD's head was spinning. "What businesses are you and Mitch involved in?"

Derrick waved his hands. "I don't want to talk about it now. Promise me you'll do what I ask. If you don't, I'll have Mitch handle it. I'm going to make sure you never have to worry about money."

"Okay," JD replied. *More lies. They just keep coming.*

"Next, step away from my case for a while. It's moving through the process. There'll be a time when I'll need your help."

JD stared at Derrick and wasn't sure what to say. She was too busy fighting to put the emotions away, if only for a little while. She could analyze this later.

"Now, tell me about your time away. Make me laugh. You were always good at that."

Fighting back fear over what she might discover as she dug deeper, she told Derrick about the three dachshunds who lived at the spa. For a short time, they laughed and escaped the hell that was their new life.

****

JD moved the salmon around the Fiesta Blue plate. Eight weeks away, she'd come back happy and positive. One visit with Derrick and the dread and stress descended like cold rain. Her self-doubts were back with a vengeance.

She tried to follow the conversation, but nothing seemed to register. The visit with Derrick had only confused her more. What she wanted was to go back in time and change everything, but it wasn't possible.

A little spark of happiness hit JD as Mitch approached the table.

"Welcome home, beautiful," Mitch said as he leaned in to gather her in his arms. He stood still, holding her at arm's length. "Let me look at you. Amazing, simply the loveliest woman in the room."

"It's good to be home. How are you?" JD enjoyed the comfort of his embrace.

"Same old thing," he said, waving his hands. "But

I'm concerned."

"About what?" JD asked.

"Something wrong with your salmon? You're playing with your food, not eating it. Would you like something else?"

"No. It's fine. I was lost in thought," she said, placing her fork on the plate.

"Gentlemen, could I borrow your lunch companion momentarily?" he asked, addressing Benjamin and Johnathan.

Johnathan's response was what JD expected. "As long as she isn't late getting back to work." His eyes danced with humor.

Mitch placed his hand on JD's elbow as she rose. "I hope you don't mind my stealing you away," he said and directed her toward the back of the restaurant.

"No problem," she said, entering his office. "I could use a distraction."

"Have a seat," Mitch said, pointing toward a red-and-black plaid wingback chair.

He sat on the footstool and locked eyes with her. "I visited with Derrick a couple of weeks ago. He asked me to speak with you."

"I know about your business dealing. He wants to liquidate some of the assets," she said.

Mitch waved his hands before taking hers. "I'm already working on it. This is something else."

"Okay." Wariness enveloped her as she tried to concentrate.

"He asked me to speak with you about the lifestyle."

JD yanked her hands away, stood, and began to pace. "Not you too! Has the world gone mad? I feel like I've crossed over into the twilight zone."

"I know it must all seem foreign to you," Mitch said, looking up.

She turned and glared at him. "Foreign? Is that what you think? Really?" She knew her tone lashed at him. She held up her hands and shook her head when he began to speak.

Disdain dripped from her words. "Let's recap, shall we." She touched her fingers as she made each point. "I've discovered the last several years of my life are based on lies. The man who loved and encouraged me is a fraud. To top it off, he likes to abuse women.

"Mitch, I only had one request when we began dating. One! To be faithful or at least have the balls to tell me if someone else came along. But no, he couldn't even do that!" She flung her hands out in despair as hot tears rolled down her cheeks.

"Hell, he probably took the lifestyle too far and is responsible for the death of the poor woman." JD's hand flew to her mouth. Derrick was responsible. There, she'd finally said what was circling in her mind for months.

Mitch reached out, but JD stepped back. She wouldn't fall apart anymore. If he held her, she would completely break down.

"I'm sorry Derrick put you in this situation." He offered her a handkerchief.

She snatched it from his fingers. Immediately recognized it as one she'd cross-stitched as a Christmas gift. "Thank you," she whispered.

"Come, sit." He motioned toward the chair. "I could say you're wrong, but you wouldn't believe me. You must come to that realization yourself. What I hope to do is help you understand the difference between love and BDSM."

"Mitch, he didn't trust me enough to talk to me, to try to explain. I'm angry he didn't ask me to take part. How bizarre is that? What is wrong with me?" JD dried her tears and blew her nose.

"There's nothing wrong with you. Anyone would be curious. You can't tell me you haven't researched the topic to death, and not just because of the case," Mitch added as he led her back to the chair.

All JD could do was nod as she felt her cheeks redden.

"Okay. Let me tell you why I think Derrick didn't invite you in. The best explanation is Freud's explanation of Madonna–whore complex. Men like Derrick view women in two categories, either saintly Madonna or debased prostitutes. He views you as his Madonna. He wants to love, spoil, and keep you safe and on a pedestal. Which I think we can both agree he did, and well."

JD couldn't find words. She opened and closed her mouth several times like a fish. Shook her head, placed her hands on her lap, and stared at Mitch.

"Derrick wouldn't debase and humiliate you by doing the things he does with other partners. He's not a sadist or a psychopath. He can feel emotions. He's a regular person who enjoys what many in society view as outside normal sexual practices."

He paused briefly before adding, "I know Derrick loves you with all his heart. You're the only woman he attempted to leave the lifestyle for. We discussed it several times."

JD let the final words drop and quietly asked, "What does he do with them, the other women?" Her stomach was churning. Like many times in the last year, she was afraid to hear the answer but had to know.

Mitch smoothed his mustache. "I've never been with Derrick during a session with a woman. It can be anything. Whatever the parties agree to. There're rules of protocol. For example, there's always a safe word. The game stops when and if the submissive wants."

"Okay," JD said and settled back in the chair. "And?"

Mitch continued as he stood and walked to his desk to retrieve a small teacup. "It can be spanking, tying up, nipple clamps, whipping, or dripping hot candle wax on the partner's body. As you already know, Derrick likes knife play, but that's a very small part."

JD dropped her head into her hands. What had Mitch said? He'd never been with Derrick when he was with a woman. Had Mitch been with Derrick? She couldn't take any more and shoved the thoughts away. When she looked up, Mitch spoke again.

"You'd be very surprised how many people you know that are part of the lifestyle in one way or another. Although most are not as extreme as Derrick." His voice shifted to sweet and soft. "There's a gala two weeks from Saturday, if you'd like to attend. It might help you understand."

JD locked eyes with Mitch. "Oh, just what I need: discover how many of our friends Derrick was with and who's laughing at me behind my back."

He took her chin in his hand. "It's a formal masquerade ball. No one would know it's you. I promise not to leave you alone for a second unless you ask me to."

Curiosity began to win over her shock and anger. "What does one wear to a BDSM gala—a leather pantsuit and a designer whip?"

Mitch chuckled and held up his hand. "I can introduce you to someone who can help with that."

JD's Ferris wheel of emotions spun again, and she smiled. "I bet you can."

"There are two rules. If you interact with someone, you must keep their secret as they'll keep yours. Anything you find will be off the record and cannot be used in Derrick's defense."

"No problem on either." JD stood and headed toward the door. She stopped, turned, and asked, "How do you have so much knowledge about this?" An uncomfortable pause rippled between them. She knew he was going to answer but was selecting his words wisely.

Mitch's mustache curved as a smile crossed his lips. "Let's say I'm the keeper of many secrets. It's the degree to which they need to be kept that makes the difference. Many people trust me to understand their situation."

JD forced a smile and headed to the table. She felt like a child with a huge secret. Maybe that was the attraction. What else would she discover on this adventure? Part of her wanted to stick her head in the sand, but something deeper drove her. She needed to discover what attracted Derrick to these sexual practices or, more important, what was lacking in her and why, again, she wasn't good enough.

Chapter Seven

JD turned slowly in front of the trifold mirror. The black, floor-length, Austrian bobbin lace gown molded to her curves. She wasn't sure what bothered her most— the plunging neckline barely keeping her breasts in place, the nonexistent back, or the front scalloped lace slit that damn near showed what Wendi called her fine china. At least the onyx pearl silk lining was almost the length of the miniskirts she'd worn as a teenager.

"Let's add the mask," Susie the tailor said, her voice almost giddy.

JD watched herself disappear behind the black crocheted mask. The iridescent shades of the blue and black peacock feathers framed the left side. A diamond pin held the plume in place.

"You look amazing. I think this is my best work ever," Susie said as she broke into a wide, open smile.

The mask secured, JD looked in the mirror, and the reflection was unrecognizable. A soft gasp of relief escaped her lips. No one would know it was her behind the mask. Now all she had to do was find the courage to walk downstairs with Mitch. Her body tingled with excitement and nerves.

As if he'd read her mind, Mitch peered over her shoulder. They were alone. She hadn't seen Susie leave. His eyes were compelling, almost magnetic.

When he didn't speak, she said, using the deep

southern accent she'd practiced over the last two weeks, "Well, do I look okay? It's the mask. The feathers have to go, right?"

"No, dear, you're perfect, and I love the accent. You need a few extra touches to put you over the top. Which is what this gala is all about—everything is over-the-top." A flash of humor crossed his face as he slid a necklace down her chest and clasped it behind her neck.

JD stroked the diamond fringe necklace. A huge stone hug between her breasts.

"It's a Victorian piece and belonged to my great-grandmother," Mitch said as he walked to face her. "The loop earrings are recreations to match," he added, placing them in her hand before slipping a bracelet on her other arm.

Her hands shook as she tried to add the earrings. "Mitch, they're beautiful, but really, this is too much."

He placed his hands on her shoulders. "Like I said, over-the-top is what we're after. Besides, it's not like my boyfriend would wear them. He prefers gold." Amusement flickered in the eyes that met hers.

"You're outrageous. It's one reason I love you," JD replied, taking the glass of champagne Mitch offered.

"I love you too, sweetie, or should I say, Mistress Lisa," Mitch said and raised his glass.

"Salute," JD said and took a sip from her glass. "Where's your mask?" JD inquired almost as an afterthought.

Mitch waved his empty hand. "Sweetheart, I'm already out. If I were any more out, I'd be one of the colorful peacocks strutting around outside showing my tail feathers."

****

Johnathan's limousine seemed to float along the lush oak canopy drive leading to the antebellum manor house. He finished the scotch and adjusted his mask. Thank goodness one of Mitch's businesses was a car service. He truly had thought of every detail.

With Mitch involved, there were never loose ends. It had always been that way since the awful night in college. Well, Johnathan wouldn't think about that. He couldn't stop the mental picture of the dead innocent girl that flashed into his mind. Why were those memories coming back now? He hadn't recalled the details like this in years. It was dead and buried. Or was it? Could someone from their past have set Derrick up?

Johnathan poured another healthy splash of scotch into the glass and studied the caramel liquid. He never quite understood the dynamics of Mitch and Derrick's relationship. Could Mitch have set their friend up?

Mitch cared a great deal about JD and would do anything to protect her. Johnathan realized JD had turned to Mitch a great deal lately. He fought back the jealousy and downed the drink in one swallow. He put the thoughts away with the glass.

The colonial revival house was the centerpiece of one of the country's oldest working plantations. Meadow Hall had continuously produced crops for more than three centuries. The residence was breathtaking, with the six large white columns and gas lanterns acting as beacons of Southern hospitality.

"Call when you are ready to head back," Joseph said as he opened the limo door.

"I will," Johnathan said, slipping a tip into the driver's hand.

"Thank you, sir," Joseph said, tipping his hat and

heading around the car.

Johnathan made his way up the stairs and slipped in the open doors. No matter the reason for a visit, Johnathan always hesitated in the foyer to enjoy the double freestanding, winding staircase. Tonight, interlaced with the mahogany spindles were ivy and black violets. The marble floors gleamed. Black orchids and deep-blue peacock feathers were displayed in cut glass crystal vases. He knew from experience the flowers had been cultivated in Mitch's greenhouse.

The other majestic centerpiece of the foyer was the chandelier. It had been fashioned in France in 1850. There were twelve cut Baccarat saucer-sized crystals sending prisms of lights and colors across the walls. Johnathan smiled, remembering the story. The antique four-and-a-half-foot crystal-and-brass fixture was winnings from a poker game. Followed by, after too much drinking, a duel over the honor of Mitch's great-great-grandmother. As he checked his top hat and coat, Johnathan smiled again and wondered if the story was true. Knowing the family's colorful history, it probably was.

He'd visited the mansion hundreds of times over the years growing up and now as a longtime friend and legal counsel. Johnathan had many fond memories in this house. Mitch was the flamboyant, first openly gay man he'd known. A smile grew on his face recalling the adventures he, Mitch, and Benjamin had growing up.

It had been Mitch who'd introduced him to the lifestyle. Johnathan had only toyed with the idea until he met Jana. She turned him on to spanking. At first, he'd been apprehensive but quickly learned it was a win-win. A firm hand on Jana's backside sent her sexual appetite soaring.

They'd been in Key West for a weekend. Jana had taken him to a club on Duval Street to watch a skit. The husband, Paul, had come home to find his wife, Louise, had broken his favorite golf club. The actor made a big production of telling how she'd been a bad girl and needed to be punished.

He'd turned Louise over his knee and slowly slid the panties down, revealing a firm, toned ass, and inspected it, squeezing and stroking every inch. Johnathan had enjoyed the punishment the actor handed down.

Since Jana moved to Japan, Johnathan hadn't taken another submissive, but toyed with the idea from time to time. Perhaps he'd take part in the submissive auction ribbon ceremony and find a willing participant. He'd bought a VIP ticket in case, but having a full-time submissive meant he'd be out to at least one woman. Maybe tonight he'd have fun and tomorrow return to his normal life.

Johnathan selected a glass of champagne from a silver tray and checked his watch. In five minutes, eight o'clock sharp, Mitch would make his grand entrance, pausing briefly on each stair for dramatic effect, making sure every eye was on him and his date. He always had an attractive man on his arm, but no one was around very long.

Perhaps there was a permanent partner, someone who couldn't be seen in public with Mitch. It was hard to know. He played his cards close to his chest. Shock hit him square between the eyes. Could it be Derrick? They were close. Could Mitch have set Derrick up? Orchestrate a murder? Johnathan shook his head and hid the inner laugh. It was ridiculous, wasn't it? Johnathan mentally filed the thoughts away to examine another time.

Mitch was the perfect host and knew how to throw a party. Johnathan wondered how many of the tuxedo-clad men and exotically dressed women he interacted with daily. Their identity was as safe as his. The masquerade gala supplied the perfect outing for those hiding in the shadows of this alternative sexual release.

He was lost in thought when a hush fell over the room. Johnathan returned his gaze to the staircase as Mitch and a woman in black descended. Her head held high, a black-gloved arm and hand atop her host's. His gaze fell to the creamy expanse of her neck around which hung a Victorian necklace. According to insurance paperwork he'd filed, it was worth more than half a million dollars. The dress appeared to cover nothing and everything at the same time. The glimpses of her toned body made his heart beat faster. The woman projected energy and power, which undeniably drew him in.

He shifted his vantage point, and what caught his complete attention was her round, firm, very spank-able ass. He'd love to take her over his knees. Would she squirm with excitement as he heated her bottom with each smack? The desire to feel the flesh of a woman's derriere under his palm was growing, as was the tightness of his slacks. There was something very therapeutic about the feel of soft skin and the sound when his palm connected with a bare bottom. The vision on the stairway was his perfect fantasy.

****

JD felt light-headed as everyone stopped talking and turned to stare. The beat of her heart drowned out the music. A flush crept up her body. She could feel the pink heat rising to her cheeks.

Mitch leaned in and whispered, "Showtime, princess, let's go."

As they descended, JD prayed she wouldn't trip and roll to the landing. At the base of her throat, a pulse beat and swelled as though her heart had risen from its usual place. What in the hell had she been thinking? This was crazy. She'd never pull it off. Everything Mitch had taught her spun in her head.

Her escort kissed her cheek and spoke in a soft voice. "You got this. What can they do, take away your birthday?"

Seeing the amusement and confidence in his eyes, she relaxed and grinned.

Halfway to the bottom, Mitch paused to address his guests. "It's a pleasure to see many of my friends tonight. Since I'm the only one without a mask, it's a guessing game as to who you are. If you're here for the bird-watcher's meeting, that's next week."

There was a round of laughter from the group. JD felt the muscles across her shoulders relax.

"Before we return to the festivities, it's my pleasure to introduce my hostess for the evening. Ladies and gentlemen, may I present Mistress Lisa."

JD wasn't expecting the round of applause before Mitch continued. "Please make yourselves at home. The gardens and gazebos are open for your enjoyment. Dinner will be served at ten. My dear," he said and escorted JD down the stairs into the ballroom.

She'd known this was coming. No one would dance until she and Mitch had. One waltz, and she'd escape for a stroll in the gardens. She slipped the small ribbon loop over her thumb, lifting the train of her dress. She'd danced here with many of their mutual friends but never in masquerade. It made it more sensual. Derrick had taught her to waltz before the first party they attended. JD gave herself a mental slap. *Don't think about him! Don't let him ruin this too.*

Mitch took her right hand in his left as the orchestra began the notes to "De Sternen Nacht." She gave way to the music and let Mitch take the lead in their journey. Around the dance floor, they moved in tandem. JD felt alive and sexy. She performed for herself as much as the crowd. She'd make Mitch proud. As the music came to a halt, the couple took a bow to a round of applause.

Amusement flickered in Mitch's eyes when they met hers. "Damn, woman, you make me wish I wasn't gay. What fun we'd have."

This time JD laughed in response. "I'm not sure either of us could stand it. I'm headed to the garden to catch my breath."

"Not sure it's going to happen," Mitch said.

"Why?" JD asked.

Before Mitch could respond, a man joined them. "Mitch, Mistress," he said with a nod.

Both responded in kind.

"Mistress, if I might be so bold as to request the pleasure of a dance?" he asked with a slight bow.

Meeting his gaze, she openly studied him and called on everything Mitch told her about the protocol. *Aloof, be aloof.* What the hell did that mean anyway? "Perhaps," she responded. From the cram session with Mitch, JD knew this tuxedo-clad man wouldn't have approached if he weren't a dominant. His request had been made in a manner to show respect for both host and hostess. She could agree or not. It was her choice.

There was something in his eyes that enticed her. JD didn't speak but simply placed her gloved hand on top of his. An electric charge seemed to pulse through her when he rested his hand on her lower back and gently moved her to him.

JD kept her shoulders straight and parallel with the floor. She noted her partner was a polished dancer as they glided around the room for most of the dance before the gentleman said, "Mistress, you're a wonderful dancer."

"You as well," she said.

"Mitch certainly knows how to throw a party."

"He's quite the host and will raise a great deal of money tonight for charity."

As the song came to an end, another man approached and requested a dance. JD agreed but regretted her decision at once. As she moved around the solarium, the sexual excitement she felt with her previous partner surged through her. She swayed to the music and fought off the guilt of wanting another man other than Derrick. Her feelings were flip-flopping again. Why couldn't she control them?

When the dance ended, she declined another, swiped a glass of champagne from a tray, and made her way to the garden to hide and breathe. Not think about the man in black and the instant connection she'd felt. What the hell was she doing here?

****

Johnathan slipped the red VIP ticket and ribbon into his pocket. The submissive auction had lost his interest. He took one last look at the scantily clad men and women who had volunteered to be part of the fundraising event tonight. He hid his grin, wondering what charity would receive the several hundred thousand dollars raised tonight. Maybe there was an old folks' home for retired mistresses and masters. He buried a laugh.

He scanned the room, looking for Mistress Lisa. He was obsessed with the mysterious woman in black. Drawn to her. Half the dance, he'd fought to keep his excitement subdued. The rest basking in her scent. It was a provocative combination of lemon and orange, but there was also a spiciness. There was something familiar about her fragrance, but he couldn't place it. Who was this exotic creature?

Johnathan spotted her chatting with Mitch, sipping wine, and watching the auction. She looked exquisite. She talked with her hands, every move sensual and inviting.

He was a novice in the lifestyle, never having considered any role but the master. Hell, he'd only had one partner. His role with Jana had been sweet and loving but still a master.

He wondered what it would be to have an experienced woman dominate him. The thought caused his heart to beat faster and his erection to grow. Would she push him to experience pain with the pleasure? There was no question he'd offer himself to her no matter the outcome.

He made his way through the crowd, but when he reached Mitch, the woman in black was gone. She'd already found someone. He was about to give up when he caught a glimpse of her on the first landing. He took the stairs two at a time and checked several open rooms before he found her in the library.

"Mistress, so this is where you've been hiding," Johnathan said.

She spoke, turning slowly, "The view is beautiful. You can see the entire garden maze."

"Yes, the view is extraordinary." Their eyes met in the mirror as he finished a head-to-toe assessment.

She grinned, nodded, and said, "Thank you."

Her response was a purr to him. She stood in a ray of moonlight. To show his intended submissive role, he said, "Mistress, if I might be permitted to ask a question?" Panic filled his mind; what if she refused?

"You may," she said, smoothing down her dress.

"I'd like to offer myself to you." She didn't respond, so he continued. "You have a beautiful neck; your shoulders call to be kissed and caressed. Makes a man want to touch you. May I?"

****

Panic was an understatement for what JD was feeling. What the hell had she gotten herself into? *Think, think, he's waiting for a response.* She drew in a sharp breath and let it out slowly. Then it hit her. The perfect answer: "If you're looking for a mistress to punish you for past indiscretions, I'm not in the right frame of mind tonight." She dismissed him with a wave of her hand like she might a fly.

"Let me please you." He'd stepped to her, and the heat of his words caressed her shoulder.

A shiver of anticipation embraced her. Her response shocked her. "Yes."

He slid an index finger to the bottom of her ear. Her excitement grew with each small circle he created with his fingertip. "Yes, so soft, so sexy," he murmured against the crook of her neck.

JD felt her nipples harden when his lips touched the nape of her neck. His tongue traced a line to the shoulder strap of her dress and returned with soft kisses, each one a bit firmer than the last. Carried away by her physical response, she was surprised by the moan of pleasure as it escaped her lips. Her nipples tingled against the silk fabric.

As his mouth feasted on her neck, his hands followed the seams of the dress, teasing the sides of her breasts. He placed small kisses along her spine, stopping when he reached fabric, and slipped his tongue under the lace. JD thought she would die of desire as he reversed his path both with his tongue and his hands. Tentatively, he slipped his hands to her breasts and fondled the rock-hard nipples. "Amazing, you taste amazing."

Her feet seemed to be floating on a cloud. She was powerless to resist. There was something wonderfully exciting about the unknown man driving her toward release. Her anticipation rose as his fingertips drew an imaginary line as he walked behind her. His hands gently slid her dress up to reveal her bottom.

"Oh my, you do have a firm, shapely ass. I thought it was tempting when it was covered. Lover perfect, tight, round, and—" His words trailed off as he used his tongue to trace a line from her waist down again. Moving her cheeks apart lightly with his tongue, tasting deeper before he moved up again.

His voice, deep and sensual, seemed to wrap her in invisible heat. The idea of his eagerness to please excited her more than she wanted to believe. Her heartbeat throbbed in her ears; her knees were weak.

He pressed against her and fondled her nipples. Even through his trousers, his erection fit perfectly between the cheeks of her ass. He whispered, "I've never been a submissive. I give myself to you completely. Tell me what you like. I'm here to serve you. You've captivated me, Mistress."

The idea of his eagerness excited her. JD fought to control her breathing. Sexual desire surged through her body. The sweet intoxicating musk of his body overwhelmed her. She was filled with a strange inner excitement as she asked, "What would you do if I were the submissive?"

****

Johnathan let out a long, slow audible breath, and his erection began to throb. He nibbled his way down her neck, giving time to calm the excitement before he whispered, "I'd take you across my knee and enjoy spanking your exceptional derriere." Her body trembled against his.

"It would be a first," she said in a whisper.

Johnathan moved to face her; he outlined her mouth with his index finger. Her chest rose and fell. "I'll be your first master, then?" he asked but with command in his voice.

Her simple nod caused his mind and body to soar.

He interlaced her fingers with his. "Come, my sweet," he said and led her to the sofa. He sat and pulled her into his arms. His searching lips found hers. The kiss wasn't what he wanted. Their masks seemed to make it impossible. But removing theirs was not an option.

Johnathan stepped back almost as if he had been shot. "Sorry, I was carried away. I forgot to ask. What's your safe word?"

"Peanuts," JD blurted out.

Johnathan chuckled and nuzzled her neck. It was as if there was a silent understanding between them. JD stood, turned, and lay across his lap. He slid the dress slowly toward her waist. Johnathan thought he'd climax with her on his lap as he stroked her ass. "Such a beautiful, firm, round bottom cries out for a spanking."

In the moonlight, he could make out a small dark area on her butt, *beauty mark or tattoo?* The thought was quickly forgotten as his excitement grew; he didn't think he'd ever been that hard.

****

JD wasn't sure what she was thinking. Here she was across a stranger's lap, wanting to be spanked. Each time his palm connected with her bottom, she felt an awakening deep inside. The swats continued in rapid succession, each one firmer than the last. With each, a feeling heated her center. Gusts of desire shook her. He rubbed her bottom gently and whispered, "Your ass is marked by my hand, but I must have all of you."

Her legs wobbled as she fought to stand. Knowing only a joining would quench the sexual blaze he'd started. When had he taken off his jacket?

"Master, how would you like me?" JD couldn't believe the lust in her voice or the game she was playing.

Johnathan brushed her cheek with the back of his hand. "Every way possible and all night if we had the time." He caressed her lips with his finger. She ran her tongue the full length of it. "Undress for me," Johnathan commanded.

JD was thrilled at the order. She lowered first one strap, then the other, and slid the dress to the floor. The mask seemed to give her a power. Tonight, she could be anyone, do anything. No one would ever know. She stood before him, wearing only five-inch black heels.

She stepped to him. "Master, may I undress you?"

He ran his fingers in her hair and whispered, "You

may."

JD kneeled before him, astonished by the fact there was no embarrassment, just pure pleasure at giving. "Please, lift your foot," she purred. One at a time, she removed his shoes and socks, stood, and stepped back. She ran her finger up his waist and unbuttoned the suspenders. She removed his cuff links, placed them on the side table, undid the buttons of his shirt, and pulled it free.

Their eyes remained locked as she removed his pants. "Master, may I touch you? I need to," JD said as her chest rose and fell in excitement.

"You may," he whispered in her ear.

She caressed his nipples with her fingertips and lips. The action drove her excitement higher.

She walked around him, pausing only slightly to caress his ass. "You have a very nice bottom yourself," she said, stroking both cheeks and moving to face him. Her eyes focused on his erection.

His gaze dropped from her eyes to her shoulders to her breasts. He swept her, weightlessly, into his arms.

JD buried her face against his throat. "Hurry, I need you inside me," she begged.

Johnathan gently lowered her to the chaise lounge. He grabbed a condom from the cobalt crystal bowl, ripped open the packet, and applied it as his tongue caressed her swollen nipples. His hand seared a path down her abdomen to her thigh.

JD caressed the curves of his back, waist, hips, and ass.

His body imprisoned her with a web of growing arousal. He tested her with three slow short strokes, then buried himself in her tight sheath. Together, they found a tempo that drove their excitement. With each deep plunge, the degree to which she responded surprised her, as did the moans of pleasure escaping her throat as the orgasm racked her body.

****

Johnathan could feel the heat of her body course down his entire length. She began to meet him stroke after stroke. Her moans drove him higher; he fought the end. More, he needed more of her.

"Good, so good," she murmured as another release claimed her body.

"Yes, my sweet, so hot, so tight, so beautiful." His words came in jagged breaths as he drove faster and faster into her as her nails marked his body. Her release felt like liquid fire as it flowed over him. Finally, he could no longer contain his response. He yielded to the burning sweetness that seemed to send him beyond the point of madness. His breaths came in long, surrendering moans.

Johnathan savored the feeling of satisfaction and wondered if she felt the same ease he did. Still connected, their bodies naked and moist from their act of lust, beneath him, she panted. He gathered her chest to his and moved, taking her with him to a seated position.

Her lips curved into a smile as she leaned in to kiss him. "The mask makes our encounter mysterious, but kissing wasn't something they were designed for."

He slid his hand under her cheeks and pulled her closer to his returning erection. She wiggled against him, rose slightly and down again. He throbbed within her; she moved higher this time. It seemed like minutes of torture passed as she lowered herself again.

His head fell back on the chair. "Sweet mother of all

things holy," he managed to say as her hot orgasm poured over him. Johnathan pulled her to him and nibbled down her neck. "You are amazing; however, as wonderful as this feels, I need a minute," he said with a chuckle.

JD kissed him on the nose, lifted herself from him, and collapsed onto the seat beside him. He heard a slight moan and smiled.

"I'll be right back." Johnathan raced to the small washroom, removed the condom, and applied another to his already-hard cock.

He caught how his partner surveyed his condition.

"Would you like me on my knees?" JD asked with a grin.

"You read my mind." He explored the soft lines of her waist, her hips, and reveled in the fact her left cheek still held a faint outline of his hand. He slid two fingers inside her heat. Her tormented groan and flow of hot release were all the invitation he needed. He joined with her again in one long stroke.

As he took her higher, he was surprised at his brazen comments. "Your ass is firm. It's very sensual watching us together."

Her reaction was to move with him. He grabbed her hips. "Yes, beautiful, come for me." As she crested, he slapped her ass.

****

JD was out of control. The hard slap to her bottom sent her hungry desire spiraling. She sensed his thrill at her reaction. She met him with uncontrolled passion. Too lost in it to be ashamed, she begged for more.

With each swat, the stranger applied more pressure. This raw sensuousness carried her higher. Even through the latex, she felt his release. His carnal moan and last slap were an act of dominance. She'd surrendered as well to his skilled hands.

Hands on her hips, Johnathan slowly withdrew and lowered her to the tufted fabric. JD wasn't sure what to do when her partner headed to the washroom. Her chest still rose and fell with each breath. Her mask was still in place, thank goodness.

She moved to the mirror and turned to check her ass. It was red and felt on fire. There were two very well-defined handprints, one on each of her cheeks. She felt the embarrassment roll over her. What did she do now? Grab her clothes and run? The reality of her actions began to sink in.

"Hello, beautiful," her partner said to her reflection in the mirror. He lightly caressed her bottom. "Sorry. I guess I got carried away." He lifted her chin until their eyes met. "You are damn reactive." He kissed her cheek, turned, and began to dress.

"No harm, no foul." *No harm, no foul? What a stupid thing to say.* What was she supposed to say? Mitch hadn't told her about this protocol. At least it made him smile. JD slipped into her dress. "I think we both played different roles tonight."

Johnathan, dressed only in his trousers, helped straighten her shoulder straps and smoothed the lace over her butt. He swatted her one more time. When she winced, he smiled. "Sorry, couldn't help myself."

JD grinned. "Damn proud of yourself, aren't you?"

He slipped his hands in his pockets as his grin grew. "Well, now that you mention it, yes. I've never been anyone's first. Mistress, did I please you?" he asked.

She was enjoying the banter, which seemed to cut

through the strangeness of the situation. She winked and slowly ran her hands from her waist over her butt. "I'd say you did very well."

He stopped buttoning his shirt and stepped toward her.

JD held up her hands. "Down, boy, no more tonight." She glanced at the clock. "Holy crap, we've been in here two hours."

"More like an hour and a half. Worried Mitch will miss you?" His grin was contagious.

"No. I'm sure he has his own game plan tonight; my attending was a favor." She stepped to Johnathan and straightened his bow tie. It seemed like the most natural thing to do—like she'd done it dozens of times.

"Thanks." He took her hands and focused his eyes on hers. "Seriously, I hope I didn't hurt you too much." When she began to speak, he placed his index finger on her lips. "I'd like to see you again." He handed her a card. "This is a safe email. Contact me if you like." Johnathan brushed his lips across her knuckles. "It was indeed a pleasure, Mistress," Johnathan said with a bow.

With that, he was gone. It was like a dream. Did it really happen? JD plopped on the chair. The pain seared through her. It did happen, and she couldn't feel more sated.

"What are you grinning about?" Mitch asked from the open doorway.

She didn't know how to respond.

"Cat got your tongue?" he asked, entering the room. "Oh, I see it now. You were swept up in the moment. Tell me all about it, and don't leave anything out," he said, pouring them both a glass of sherry.

"Good girls don't kiss and tell."

"Tonight, it appears you have teen a very bad girl. So, tell me." Mitch handed her a glass.

"Let's say I have some firsthand knowledge." She rubbed her butt.

Both roared with laughter.

Chapter Eight

JD sipped her wine and stared at the bright white rectangular business card with rounded edges. One single line of black print, an email address, so simple. She used electronic mail every day, a few keystrokes, and *whish*, the message was on its way.

The damn card. She'd tossed it in the trash but panicked at the thought the press might find it.

She marched into her office a dozen times over the past weeks to shred it but couldn't do it. She wanted to email her mystery master. Her body ached for another encounter, but that meant coming out. She couldn't do it. Not now, probably never, but what harm could one email cause.

She ran her hands through her hair and swirled the wine in her glass. Okay, she'd send one message.

Panic hit again. What email address would she use? She couldn't use her office or private email. JD let her head drop to the table. Damn Mitch for talking her into going to the gala. This was his fault, entirely!

JD checked her watch: seven thirty. Mitch, she could talk to Mitch. She slipped the card into the pocket of her jeans, grabbed her purse, and headed for the garage.

She was in the car and headed for the Corner Table before she realized she had left without checking her makeup. She heard Derrick's disapproving voice in her head but shut it down. She parked, checked her lipstick, took a deep breath, exited the car, and handed the keys to the valet.

"Good evening, Ms. Ellis," the young man said.

"Hello, Sam," she said, reading his name tag.

JD marched past the hostess stand and scanned the restaurant. Her stomach was churning. What in the hell was she thinking? Barging in without so much as a phone call. She'd lost her mind. She'd calmly turn around, walk down the steps, and ask for her car.

"JD," a very familiar mellow voice floated across the room. It was Mitch, thank goodness.

"I didn't see you on the reservation list," Mitch said as he folded her in his arms.

"I don't have a reservation. I'm sorry, I'll go. This was a bad idea. I have to go," she stammered. There was a tightness in her chest. Her neck, ears, and face felt hot.

"Nonsense." He kissed her cheek, took her hand, and led her to the bar. "White wine?" he asked as JD slipped onto the stool.

"In a bucket, please." JD tried to laugh but couldn't hide begging in her tone.

In seconds, a full cut-crystal glass was placed in front of her. "To what do I owe the honor of a visit from my favorite lady?" Mitch asked, patting her hand.

JD played with the cocktail napkin, took a sip of wine, and looked at the heavens for guidance. "I need your help," she whispered.

A grin grew on Mitch's face. "Anything within my power is yours," he said, placing his elbows on the mahogany surface, linking his fingers, and leaning in.

JD relaxed a bit, took a gulp of wine, and smiled. "It's personal, very personal."

Mitch lifted the pass-through and held out his hand. "Sounds mysterious, let's go to my office."

He took her hand. "Come with me." As they walked toward his office, JD glanced to her left and saw Johnathan sitting at a table with a very beautiful young woman. Her temper flared as an instant heat overtook her.

"She's a niece from out of town," Mitch said as if he'd read JD's mind.

"What? Johnathan's only my friend," JD blurted out.

"Okay," Mitch said as he opened the office door. "My mistake."

What the hell was wrong with her? Johnathan was a friend. Where had the white-hot flash of jealousy come from?

"Have a seat and tell me what I can do to help," Mitch said, pointing to the sofa.

JD took a deep breath, emptied the glass in one swallow, and placed her glass on the table. "At the gala. I, well, you know, I…" she trailed off.

"You met someone?" Mitch filled the dead air as he poured more wine into her glass.

JD felt her cheeks redden. "Yes. He gave me a card with an email address, just an email," she said, reaching for her wine.

"And you want to know who he is?" Mitch said, crossing his legs.

"No. Oh, hell no! I want to email him. I know it's crazy," she said. She stood and began to pace. "It's like an obsession. How can I love Derrick yet crave this other man with every inch of my being? Is this what it was like for Derrick?" JD asked and plopped on the sofa.

Mitch chuckled and stroked his mustache. "There's the conundrum. Is it the interaction or the fact it is forbidden? Which makes you want more?"

Before she could answer, Mitch stood, walked to his desk, and sat. "You need a safe email address, and I, my dear, can make it happen." He continued to talk as his fingers worked the keyboard. "My system is encrypted. It's a virtual private network. Both are fairly new technology; I venture to guess it is tighter than your law firm."

"Mitch, I'm glad you're my friend," JD said, and sipped her wine.

"Same, back at you." Mitch's tone turned serious as the printer beside his desk began to hum. "Like the gala, this is a secret to be guarded. You must type in the web address each time. Do not save it to your browser."

"Okay," JD replied. Then asked, "Why do you trust me?"

Mitch took the paper from the printer and turned to face her. He placed his hand on her shoulder. "You and I are alike; our souls recognize each other. Like me, you know in your gut who you can trust. Not very often, but occasionally, someone slips through our walls. On the outside, we seem fine, but we find our revenge in due time."

A cold chill ran down JD's spine. There was more to this man than she'd imagined. There was a deep hurt and pain here; the same with her. "Are you talking about Derrick?"

Mitch took her chin in his palm and lifted it until their eyes met. "Wow, we certainly took a dark turn." He folded the paper in half twice and handed it to JD. "I meant, in general, people hurt us. We're down for a while, but we bounce back. We need more wine. How about I treat you to dinner?"

JD tried to put the thought in her mind that Mitch had said too much and was backpedaling. "Sounds wonderful. Have I told you lately I love you?"

Mitch let out a loud laugh. "If only I were straight." He kissed her on the cheek and whispered, "I love you too. I'm here for you. No matter what, you can always come to me."

JD knew he meant it with all his heart, and he understood her like no other.

"So, do you want a steak?"

"No. I want a bowl of cheese grits and a side of pecan-crusted fried okra."

"I love a woman who's a cheap date," Mitch said, reaching for her hand.

As Mitch pulled out her chair, JD couldn't shake the feeling there were many things about Derrick her host knew. The question was, with time, would he share them?

****

JD smiled, looking at her new home. It suited her more than the showplace on Lake Ella. Her home—much better than the showplace on Lake Ella, with its glitz and glam meant to impress, not a real home.

This house felt happy and welcoming. The camellia trees and a showstopping Japanese magnolia set off the front yard. The remodel had taken months, but everything was done. Well, except for the powder room toilet, but she'd do the repair.

As if on cue, Johnathan pulled into the driveway. JD waved and held back a laugh when she saw the scowl as he climbed out of the car and stomped to the trunk.

"Here," he said, handing JD the bags. "This is the last time I go to the hardware store for you."

"It isn't like you'd never been to a hardware store," JD said. She saw the look on his face and chuckled. "Oh, my, it was." After a burst of laughter, she continued, "You'll be ready for a flannel shirt by Christmas." JD noticed Johnathan almost shuddered.

"I don't do flannel shirts."

JD tried not to laugh but couldn't help herself. "I love them to sleep in. Keeps everything all warm." JD looked inside one of the bags. "All I needed was a toilet float and valve; that's what I told you."

"I know. 'Stop and pick up a toilet float and a valve,' you said. Like I'd know what the hell they were. The hardware store salesman saw me coming, and well, there it is."

JD doubled over laughing. "Sorry. I should've gone myself. Thanks, I'm sure it will all come in handy one day. What do you think of the stone flower beds?"

"Beautiful, the multicolor azaleas set off the front yard. I still don't understand why you bought a place with multiple projects and this far out."

"It's Lake Bradford, not outer Mongolia, twenty minutes to the office, and I love the privacy. I have all this room," she said, turning in a circle, "my own dock and boathouse. We can go fishing. I understand there're largemouth bass and brim aplenty."

"Oh yeah, fishing. I can't wait."

JD slipped her arm in Johnathan's. "I'll bait your hook."

Johnathan looked at his watch. "I think my cat has a shampoo appointment."

"Like you would have a cat. You're such a city

boy."

"I am not. I know how to fish and repair stuff."

"Sure, you do, says the man who got soaked at the hardware store. What you have is a repairman, Alex, a maid, Laura, and an outstanding gardener, Julius—all who must have the patience of Job to work for you."

Johnathan laughed. "You forgot the pool boy, Paul."

"Come on, spoiled brat. I'll buy you a beer and give you the nickel tour. I've completed several projects since your last visit."

"What about the toilet repair?"

"I'll get to it."

JD entered the front door, sat on the church pew, and removed her boots.

"Still shoes-off zone?" he asked.

"No, I've got others for out back. Come check out the office. I decided to leave the wood-burning fireplace and wood beams. I think they add character."

"Where did you find the furniture?"

"Mitch took me to an auction in Monticello. Found them, my bedroom suite, and the dining furniture in the sunroom." JD walked toward the kitchen. "What's your pleasure, Counselor?"

"Beer works. I thought you were crazy having navy lower cabinets, but it works."

"I went for something a bit more modern but at the same time relaxed. Mitch insisted on top-of-the-line stainless steel appliances and quartz countertops. I think he drove the contractors crazier than I did."

"Oh, I remember the never-ending discussions about the tile for the backsplash, laundry room, and bathrooms. He was at the office with samples so often some people thought he'd become a decorator."

"Oh, stop, we had a great time " JD handed him a beer. "Come on, let me show you outside; it's my dream spot." She led him through the open French doors to a large brick patio. "Doesn't this view whisper peace and tranquility? Take a minute, listen to the wind chimes and birds."

"It is beautiful. I'll give you that "

"Check out the gazebo. I took your suggestions and went with a cedar stain; of course, the screens are new."

"I don't remember there being screens, and where did the forest go?" Johnathan joked.

"Sit down, smart-ass, and enjoy the view. Julius came out and found satsuma, red and white grapefruit, key lime, kumquat, banana, and Myer lemon trees. He recommended a guy who cleared out the bad stuff."

"The huge lot with the oak trees calls for backyard get-togethers. Guess I know where the next firm picnic will be."

"We can make it happen. Let's take a walk."

Johnathan sipped his beer and moved toward the lake bank. "Look, there's a bald eagle circling the lake, hunting for its dinner."

Tongue-in-cheek, JD said, "Careful, there may be Florida panthers and black bears protecting their wood habitats bordering the water."

Johnathan quickly looked to his left and then turned to face JD. "You're just plain cruel sometimes."

JD sipped her beer. "You want to see the workshop? What man doesn't love power tools?" JD asked with a wink.

****

Johnathan picked a rocking chair on the workshop porch, and JD joined him. He took a draw on his beer and enjoyed the gentle sound of the water caressing the shoreline. A pair of cardinals nibbled from the birdfeeder. Hummingbirds moved from feeder to flowers. "How are you doing?"

"Okay, I guess." After a long pause, JD continued, "Remodeling the house gave me a positive focus."

"Where you going to hide now?" Johnathan asked, continuing to rock, not turning to look in her direction.

"Right now, get more beer," JD said, standing.

He reached out and took her hand. "It can wait; let's talk."

"About what?"

"You. I'm worried; hell, we're all concerned about you."

JD dropped back in her chair and stared at the water. "I don't know, Johnathan. I'm mentally all over the place. I feel guilty, stupid, used, and want to run away."

He sat in silence as tears stained her cheeks, and she spoke. "I gave everything to our relationship and believed Derrick was different. My life growing up was horrible. My mother was a prostitute, and my father was a pimp and drug dealer. But he took care of me, made sure I went to school, and never hurt me. It wasn't until I was ripe that I understood I'd been nothing more than a long investment. I was a virgin to be sold on the black market, so I ran away."

"JD, I had no idea." This was foreign to Johnathan. He couldn't imagine growing up in that environment.

"It's okay, really." JD waved her hands. "I'm telling you because it's how my life has been. I trust people, and they use and disappoint me. I told Derrick honesty was all I needed, especially if someone else came along, he'd tell me. It was the one thing I asked. He said he would never cheat or lie to me. I even told him never say never, but he said I could believe him, and like a fool, I did."

Johnathan wanted to take her in his arms, tell her everything would be okay but knew he couldn't. Derrick was in real trouble, but he was too. He loved JD but couldn't go there right now. He stood and placed his hands on her shoulders. "I don't know what's going to happen, but we'll get through this. No matter what happens, I'll always be here for you."

JD collapsed into his arms and sobbed. Johnathan held tight as her body shook. Over the top of her head, he saw Mitch and Benjamin approaching. He held up one hand, and the pair returned to the house.

"It will turn out the way it's supposed to. What's done cannot be undone," JD said, stepping back and wiping the tears away. "Let's open a couple bottles of wine. Mitch and Benjamin will be here soon," JD said, stepping back.

"There they are now," Johnathan said, pointing toward the patio.

"I must look a mess," JD said, pulling a bandanna from her jeans pocket. She wiped her face and blew her nose.

"Perhaps you are allergic to something in the yard?" Johnathan suggested and smiled.

"Thanks for being my friend. I can always count on you." She stopped and turned to face him. "Promise to tell me the truth no matter how mad or hurt you think I might be."

"I promise, but remember, Derrick's my client, and if he asks me not to divulge something, I can't."

"Okay, I can live with that. Let's go see what Mitch brought for dinner. We can drink wine and howl at the moon like wolves."

"Oh, now you have wolves too," Johnathan said, laughed, and took her hand.

****

"Give me a minute. I want to fill the birdfeeders and close up the barn," JD said, releasing his hand.

"Okay, but don't take too long. I'm sure Mitch brought something yummy."

"I need to clear my head a bit. I won't be long, I promise," JD said, crossing her heart.

Working with her hands gave JD time to bury the emotions racing once again through her body with her blood. Would there ever be a time when she would feel like herself again? But who was that really? She hadn't a clue. So much of her was tied up to the person Derrick modeled her to be. That's what he had done. Made her the perfect lady to show off. A partner he could brag about, be on his arm at the events, entertain without mistake, dress as he liked, and control. The sudden realization hit her as hard as a fist. She fell back on a bale of hay.

She felt the panic attack beginning at her toes and marching up her body. She removed the pill bottle from her pocket and popped an anxiety pill. *Breathe, breathe, you can stop this. Don't let him win anymore.*

By the time she headed back, JD was in control. She watched the three men on the porch: Mitch, Johnathan, and Benjamin. They looked so serious. Two years ago, it would have been the four of them sharing secrets, the secrets of their circle. They were thick as thieves and had been since college. She would have been too oblivious to everything. What confidences did they have? Could the three of them know more about Derrick's other life

100

than they were saying?

JD shook her head and plastered a smile on her face. She looked at everyone through suspicious eyes now. She'd have a drink and dinner and attack the topic tomorrow. *Keep your friends close and your enemies closer,* flashed in her mind. That made her smile. After all, who could she really trust? Was anyone who they said they were?

Chapter Nine

JD drummed her fingertips on her left thigh. As she'd expected, and Johnathan had warned, she'd be interviewed again. The case was moving closer to trial, and the prosecutor was covering all the bases.

It would all go fine; Johnathan was at her left. He knew all her secrets. Well, most of them. JD licked her lips, recalling Mitch's gala and her temporary lapse of judgment, but it had been unbelievably exciting. The most out of character thing she'd ever done.

A wave of sexual heat rolled over her. She closed her eyes and was back in the library. The masked stranger caressed her neck and shoulders. Between kisses, whispering his desire. Every inch of her had ached for release.

He may have taken her hard and fast, yet she'd never felt more satisfied and wanted more as her lover disappeared from the room and her life. It was purely the most sensual experience of her life. A smile crept over her lips, remembering the business card hidden in her underwear drawer and the cryptic sexual emails they'd exchanged.

"You okay?" Johnathan asked.

"Sure, why?" she asked.

"You're flushed," he said, placing his hand over hers. "It'll be okay. Questioning you again is only a formality. The prosecution doesn't want any surprises at trial. Your alibi is airtight."

JD chuckled and turned to him. "Right, I was home alone, sleeping. We'd never be satisfied with that answer from a client's girlfriend. We'd be up her butt with a microscope."

"They want to make sure we don't use you as an alternative suspect."

"I know. It's just—" Before she could finish, two detectives entered the room.

JD smiled at Mac.

"Hello, JD, Johnathan. This is Detective Hopkins. He's working the case with me." The group exchanged handshakes and sat around the table.

"JD, thanks for coming in."

"I'd like to say no problem, but I have clients this afternoon." JD looked at her watch. Her schedule was clear, but she wanted this short and sweet.

Mac turned on the recorder. "Would you state your name for the record again?"

"Jennifer Dianne Ellis."

"What is your profession?"

"Attorney."

"We're here today to discuss the murder of Megan Ferguson. Do you have any knowledge of this crime?"

"Yes." JD wanted to smile at the way the two detectives looked at each other. She let the silence hang.

"Could you elaborate?" Mac asked.

Johnathan spoke. "Ms. Ellis is part of the defense team for Derrick August. Any conversations about the alleged murder are protected under client-attorney privilege. Do you have another line of questions? If not, we'll be on our way." Johnathan began to rise.

"I do have a few questions," Detective Hopkins said,

locking eyes with JD.

"Okay," Johnathan said.

"Other than being part of the defense team, what's your current relationship with Mr. August?"

"As I stated in my earlier interview, we were engaged. At this point, I'm part of his legal team." She held up her bare left hand, showing no ring.

"Did you have knowledge of Mr. August's deviant sexual activities prior to him becoming your client?"

Johnathan touched JD's hand before answering for her. "Please define deviant sexual activities."

Mac leaned back in the chair. JD saw the frustration building, as she was sure Johnathan had as well.

"Were you aware Mr. August was involved with others outside your relationship?"

JD looked to Johnathan and spoke quietly, "It appears there were many areas of Mr. August's life to which I was unaware. His sex life was one."

"Do you have keys to the residence in which the murder occurred?"

"Detectives, let me make this easy for you," Johnathan said. "My client was half owner of the property and stayed there many times, alone and with Mr. August. Yes, she has keys, as do any number of people, such as the rental agency, past renters, cleaning staff, and the security company. I might have one in my desk. The last time Ms. Ellis was in the cottage was approximately three weeks before the murder."

Before either detective could speak, he continued, "During my client's first interview, she provided DNA and fingerprints. Which you certainly found at the crime scene given her ownership. She has no first-hand knowledge regarding the murder."

JD noticed Mac's attempt to interrupt by raising his hand, but Johnathan kept talking. "All this was discussed previously, but for the record, I'll recap. On the night in question, my client was home. We have supplied medical, home security, cell phone records, and a host of documented information without a warrant. Do you have any additional questions or discovery requests?"

"Not at this time," Mac said as he reached to turn off the recorder.

Johnathan picked up his briefcase and stood. "Ms. Ellis has gone out of her way to cooperate with this investigation. Mac, any other questions come through me. Got it?"

"Sure."

"Let's go; we're done here." Johnathan said to JD.

JD's thoughts spun as they entered the elevator. Did they suspect her? Think she helped Derrick with the murder or murdered the poor girl herself? There had to be an answer. There's no such thing as a perfect murder. Or is there?

"You okay?" Johnathan asked as the elevator door closed.

"Could they possibly think I killed her? That I knew about his other life? You've seen the pictures. How could anyone in their right mind have done that?" Desperation filled her voice. "Do you think Derrick's the killer?"

"It doesn't matter what I think," Johnathan said. As the elevator doors opened, he removed the key fob from his pocket.

She placed her hand on his arm and turned to face him. "What you think matters to me," JD said.

"This isn't the place for a conversation. Let's go to Mitch's, get a private room, and talk."

JD's stomach turned at the thought of Derrick facing lethal injection. What if they couldn't find an answer? A shiver snaked down her spine when within a very small place in her heart, a voice boomed. *He deserves to die, the lying son of a bitch.*

****

Mitch greeted the couple when they entered the crowded restaurant. "You two look like you could use a drink."

"That's an understatement," JD replied as she looked around the room. She knew the gossip mill was churning. Professionally, she was unshakable. Personally, she was humiliated. People had to be wondering if she was part of the BDSM lifestyle. Did they think Derrick was guilty? Or she was somehow involved? Pain hit as she recalled the gala. What if her involvement was revealed? Dread set in again. She hated the revolving door of emotions that assaulted her daily.

"We definitely need a drink and someplace to talk," Johnathan said.

"No problem. Scotch on the rocks?" Mitch asked.

JD felt like she was swimming in cotton as Mitch led them to the back of the restaurant. No amount of booze or time would fix this. She sat in the chair Johnathan pulled out, placed her head in her hands, and let the tears flow. It wasn't supposed to be like this.

****

Johnathan sat across from JD, nursing his drink and listening to her sob. What could he do? What would he tell her? How could he explain without letting her know he was part of the same group as Derrick? But it wasn't the same; Derrick took pleasure in inflicting pain, albeit with willing partners. But hadn't he spanked the beautiful woman at the gala until his handprint was visible, very visible? He'd hoped she remembered him every time she sat for days. Even now, weeks later, her response still aroused him. Their emails were full of sexual fantasy. If only they could meet again.

"Sorry about the tears. You want to order something to eat?" JD asked, drying her tears and lifting her drink.

"What?" Johnathan replied.

"Do you want to order something to eat? We worked through lunch."

"Sure," he said, realizing Mitch was standing at their table.

"What do you recommend?" JD asked.

"How about grilled Greek grouper? Fresh off the boat this afternoon."

"Sounds good," Johnathan said.

"Me too, and surprise us with the sides."

"Will do."

When they were alone, JD asked, "Did you know about any of this?"

"No. I thought the special today was prime rib." Johnathan didn't get the smile he'd hoped for. "So much for a job as a comedian," he said and tried a smile. JD didn't respond but simply stared into his eyes. Damn, he wouldn't want her cross-examining him. He sipped his drink as a stalling tactic.

"Did you know about the BDSM activities?" JD asked.

"I'd heard rumors," he finally answered, staring into his drink.

"You never thought to say anything to me." The anger in her voice came through loud and clear.

Her response made him angry, and he didn't temper

his answer with good sense. "What was I supposed to do? Walk into your office and say, hey JD, so are you into the tie-me-up, make-me-write-bad-checks kind of kinky sex? Or perhaps, take you over my knee and spank you good and hard. See if you asked for more?"

This time when their eyes met, JD's response began as a giggle but turned into a strong laugh. She held up both hands in an attempt to stop his scowl. "Okay, I see your point," JD said between snickers.

Johnathan drew in a long breath; he'd dodged a bullet. Why in the hell had he mentioned spanking her? He knew full well, more times than not, when he walked behind this gorgeous lady, it had crossed his mind. She had an amazing ass. Spanking her was a fantasy he enjoyed regularly. Puzzled, he recalled the only time he hadn't thought about her was at the gala. The Mistress had his full attention.

JD's voice turned serious. Her question came out in a small, sad whisper, "Johnathan, do you think Derrick's the killer?"

He reached across the table and took her hand. "I'm not sure. If someone set him up, they needed a great deal of information and perfect timing. So many details to work out. Nothing could be left to chance. There're numerous questions, like why he turned off the video surveillance."

"He said he didn't want to forget to delete it. Afraid I'd see the video. What's wrong with me? Why wasn't I enough?"

"I'm not sure how to answer."

"Mitch told me it was something Derrick could only control for a while. Like an alcoholic, I guess. Had to have the fix. Vanilla sex wasn't enough. I guess I'm the only person who didn't know about vanilla sex. Sounds like I'm frigid and unexciting."

"That isn't what it means at all," Johnathan said and at once began to panic as JD's face turned bright red.

Even though they were in private, she leaned in and whispered, "You know about vanilla sex?"

Johnathan began slowly measuring every word. He didn't want to lie, but he could prevaricate. "I've heard the word tossed around. I'm not really sure when I picked it up and the meaning." *It's close enough to the truth,* he told himself as he sipped his drink. He was very happy when a waiter knocked on the door and entered with their meal.

JD sipped her drink and didn't speak until the food was placed in front of them and the waiter had left. "Was Derrick into this in college?" she asked, cutting into her fish. When he didn't respond, she looked up and continued, "The four of you were fraternity brothers and then roommates. You have to have some idea."

Johnathan was headed down a slippery slope. "Back then, I knew he was into light bondage. I honestly thought he'd given it up, or you were into it. It isn't a topic discussed during a golf game. I had no idea he'd gotten into the darker side." Johnathan was pleased with the knowledge Derrick hadn't spoiled JD with his games.

JD ate several bites before she continued, "I'm sorry, Johnathan, I have no right to pry. I know you are only trying to help. Thanks for talking to me. I won't ask about this again."

"It's okay," he responded between bites. At least he hoped the subject was closed. JD would probably leave the firm if she discovered he was into spanking. At least he still had the fantasy of JD across his lap, her exceptional, bare ass fiery red from a spanking. He rubbed his fingertip across his palm to calm the growing desire. His erection throbbed, reminding him he needed a release.

He'd be his own sexual partner again or perhaps contact Lisa and see if she would like to meet. Their sexual messages would have to be enough until the trial was over. For now, he'd live in his own fantasy world. How sad was that?

Chapter Ten

JD leaned against the table and stared at the evidence board. At one point, it was covered with pictures of Derrick's women and other possible suspects. Thoughts of the murder didn't have the same emotion they once did. Perhaps she was still in shock or simply didn't care anymore. The problem was she couldn't figure out which was true.

There'd been almost as many business associates' pictures posted. Ones he'd screwed over, but each had been eliminated, not even one with a shaky alibi. Another thing she learned, Derrick was a dishonest man who had no morals or ethics when it came to his business ventures.

One alternative suspect, someone to build a defense around, was all they needed. JD rubbed her sweaty palms on her navy linen pants. "It is time to think outside the box," she said to the empty room. Her mind drifted back to her thoughts about Derrick's friends.

"JD, you wanted to see me?"

"Mr. Drake, thanks for coming up, have a seat," she said to the firm's head investigator.

"It's Paul," he said, closing the door before sitting in the chair across from JD.

"Thanks for coming up. I have a rather delicate question to ask," she said, tapping her pen against her desk.

"Ask; I'm a vault."

"Have you double-checked everyone in Derrick's inner circle?" She made direct eye contact as she asked.

"Johnathan told me to run everyone, including himself and you. There were some blips but nothing that led anywhere. I'm still digging," Paul said.

"Thanks for coming by and the honesty," JD said as Paul rose to leave the office.

"No problem, I'll keep you posted," he said before opening the door.

She sat and began to doodle on the yellow legal pad. Was there something in Derrick's past Paul missed? It was time to do a deeper dive. She should've thought of it before.

She'd start with college. Johnathan would've told her if there'd been a reason to investigate there, wouldn't he? Her street smarts were on high alert. The man who'd sworn to love her had lied, cheated, and used her for years. She might as well have been his trained monkey used to charm people. They'd been the perfect couple. What a fool she had been.

Who else in the circle of friends wasn't who they professed to be? Mitch obviously had secrets. Who could she trust?

JD logged into her computer, mentally did the math, and went back even further. One cup of coffee after another, she scanned newspaper articles through high school and to college. Searching for deaths, police raids, drug arrests, and anything out of place. The more unusual, the better.

"I've got the motions and letters you dictated," Wendi said, placing files on JD's desk.

"Thanks, sorry about the boatload of work," JD said,

smiling at her assistant.

"I'd rather be busy. Plus, it's good to see you back in the game. I'm heading out to pick up lunch; you want something?"

"I would, matter of fact. If you fly, I'll buy. How about butternut squash soup, mixed greens salad, and pecan pie from Corner Table?"

"I can't pass that up. I'll go by the bank and swing by the restaurant," Wendi said.

"I'll call Mitch. Pickup in forty-five minutes work?"

"Cool, I'll be back."

JD placed the order and crawled back into her research. She was about to give up when a headline caught her attention: "College Junior Dies in Freak Accident." She scanned the article, selected the text, and hit Print. By the time Wendi arrived with lunch, JD was reading the police report she'd sweet-talked a Boston Police sergeant into emailing.

****

JD watched the men sitting around her dining table. They'd laughed and talked over a meal like this many times. But tonight, her plan was to lure them into a false sense of security with wine, baked spaghetti, salad, garlic bread, and now the final act, carrot cake and Irish coffee.

"JD, this was a great idea. Thanks for having us over. The new house is really coming together," Johnathan said.

"Thanks. This really feels like home," JD said, serving cake to each of her guests. "I have to thank Mitch for teaching me to cook. If not for him, we'd be eating takeout."

"I can arrange that anytime, but my dear, this meal was amazing," Mitch said before taking a bite of cake.

"Thanks, but I wasn't completely honest about the reason for this impromptu gathering. I have some questions. Beginning with who's Jess Morgan, and why didn't one of you tell me about her?"

JD saw shock register on all three men's faces; she'd blindsided them. They looked at each other, but Benjamin spoke, "What about Jess?"

"That's what I want to know. She fell out a window of your fraternity house, and the cause of death was undetermined. From what I've been able to find, the investigation was simply dropped. Witness statements, evidence—everything except a vague police report and one page of the autopsy disappeared. Is it possible this could be connected to Derrick's situation?"

"Jess was one of the fraternity's little sisters. We had six or eight. They acted as hostesses, took care of things at parties, and watched over the house," Johnathan said before taking a bite of cake.

"I got this," Mitch said to his companions. "Jess was my girlfriend. Society wasn't as forgiving as they are now. I loved her or thought I did. I even tried to go straight. We didn't have sex. We spent time together. She said I was the first guy who treated her nice." Mitch paused and took a sip of coffee.

"So, what happened the night she died? Were you with her?" JD asked.

Johnathan answered. "There was a frat party. We were all there. I didn't think Jess did drugs, but that night she did. Something went wrong. She was high and fell out of an open window."

"Was she alone in the room?"

The pause told her the answer before Benjamin spoke. "No. Well, she'd been with Derrick, but he left before she fell."

"Did he get her high to get her into bed? Did he rape her? Are you sure he didn't push her out the window?" JD shoved back from the table and ran her hands through her hair as she paced. She stopped, turned, and stared at the men. "What the hell? You didn't think this was important to bring up? What if it comes out at trial? Is there someone from her past who could've been stalking Derrick, set this up?"

"Before we knew Jess had fallen, Derrick came downstairs looking for her. He said they had some fun, he went to the bathroom, came out, and she was gone," Johnathan said.

"That's the truth. If we," Mitch said, looking from man to man, "thought it was anything else, we'd have told the cops."

"There's no mention of any of you in the report I received."

Mitch raised his hand. "That's on me too. Jess and her mother, Anna, went home with me for spring break about a month before the accident. My dad went to see Anna after, took care of the funeral arrangements, and followed up with the police. We never heard anything else about it."

"Mitch, if Jess was your girlfriend, why was she having sex with Derrick?"

"I thought she was gay too, we weren't having sex, and we hung out all the time. Derrick said she approached him. Since he knew about my sexual orientation, he thought it was cool. He swore he didn't know she was high," Mitch said and dropped his head to his hands.

"We thought she left. It was a couple of hours before

she was discovered," Johnathan said.

"I called the police; they investigated," Benjamin added.

"Why was the death ruled undetermined?" JD asked Johnathan.

"I guess it couldn't be determined if she fell, jumped, or was pushed. The only thing Dad told me was Anna didn't want it ruled a suicide, because Jess couldn't have a burial mass or be buried on Catholic consecrated ground," Mitch said.

Johnathan picked up the story. "We graduated a few weeks later and moved into a house my parents owned. Ben and I went to law school; Derrick and Mitch worked on their MBAs. We never really talked about it. It was easier, I guess. We were all young."

"Do you think there was more to it, and that's why none of you wanted to talk about it?" JD asked, glancing from man to man.

"I don't know," Mitch said.

"I think it was easier to let it go," Benjamin added.

JD sipped her coffee and stared at Johnathan. Setting her cup aside, she said, "Nothing to say, Counselor?"

"I've got plenty to say. As for the topic at hand, I think we've covered it. The rest I'll save until we're alone."

"Really, well, how convenient," JD replied sharply. Her stomach churned, and she felt her face redden.

"What I've got to say is between us and has nothing to do with Jess. You got a problem with that, Counselor?"

JD could feel the anger radiating off Johnathan. "I apologize if I crossed a line. Shall we finish our dessert?"

"I need to get back to the restaurant," Mitch said. He

kissed JD's cheek and whispered, "See you tomorrow for brunch. Love you."

"Okay," JD said, handing Mitch his scarf.

"I'm parked behind Mitch. I guess I'll be going too," Benjamin said and hugged JD.

JD closed the door and turned to face Johnathan.

He took two steps toward JD. "What the hell were you thinking?"

"You didn't tell me about this. I wanted to see the reactions and get to the truth. If Derrick has killed before—"

Johnathan held up his hand. "Just shut up! Do you realize how stupid that sounds? We're your friends, and in case you forgot, two of us are your bosses. Do you think so little of us? We wouldn't have lied to protect Derrick if we even suspected he'd killed Jess. Thanks for the insult and lack of trust," he said, picking up his jacket.

JD reached out and touched Johnathan's arm, but he pulled away. "You taught me everything's on the table until evidence rules it out. Perhaps I didn't think my approach through."

"Damn straight, you didn't. I know you're crazy in love with Derrick and would do anything to get him off, but accusing and slandering the people who've always been there for you? Really, JD?"

"Why didn't you tell me?" she asked.

"There was no reason, plus plausible deniability if you're called to testify, and because I'd already checked into the family. Anna passed away five years ago; there's no other family. All you had to do was trust me and ask. I'm not a liar. If you don't know that by now, I don't know any other way to prove it. Decide which way it is.

If you can't look me in the eyes and tell me you do, I'll expect your resignation on my desk Monday morning." Johnathan brushed by JD, grabbed his coat, and slammed the door behind him.

JD's hands shook as she gathered up cups and plates and carried them to the kitchen. She'd lost her objectivity; dammit, Johnathan was right, again. When had the doubt and distrust of everyone begin? She was grasping at straws to find anything to give Derrick a fighting chance. Many lies and secrets had been revealed. There could be more. She needed to stop digging. Derrick had ruined her life, but hadn't she allowed him to do that? What more could there be? She rinsed each dish and placed it in the dishwasher.

The panic attack hit like lightning. Sweat soaked her clothes. The room began to spin. Her pulse thundered. JD tried to hold on to the sink, but the trembling in her hands traveled down into her arms and legs. Giving way to the unsteadiness, she sank to the floor. Her heart seemed to gallop faster and faster. Breathing seemed impossible. She fought for every shallow gasp of air.

"You are dying," a small voice whispered as her vision grew darker and her sight became a kaleidoscope of stars. "This is what death feels like, and you're going to die here alone. Derrick has taken everything. Now you are giving him your life."

JD had no idea how much time passed as she fought her way back to reality. The blackness had taken over, seemed to drain away her life.

She crawled to the sofa and sank into the pillows. What was this hold Derrick had over her that caused her to do such awful things? JD had allowed herself to be powerless, but that had to stop now. She'd said it before, but it was time for action and to find her way back. Derrick would most likely be convicted, and there was nothing she could do. It was time to accept the situation and do damage control. JD was taking her life back!

****

JD ate crow along with her eggs Benedict. The dish was one of her favorites, but today it tasted like dust. Even the cool mimosa did nothing to soothe her dry throat. She apologized to Benjamin; he'd been more than gracious. Mitch hugged her and whispered they would talk later.

The first time in a long time, she could recall, Johnathan did not attend the Sunday brunch at the Corner Table. This was where they'd met for the first time, she'd been nervous, and they'd been so nice. JD took a deep breath and beat herself up a little more inside. Look how she had repaid them.

JD jumped when Mitch touched her shoulder.

"Let's take a walk in the garden," he said.

"Okay," JD said. She was sure he was going to let her have it with both barrels. "Did Johnathan call?" she asked, trying to make conversation as they took the ramp to the small garden.

"No. But I'm sure it'll be fine," Mitch said, taking her hand and kissing it.

"I really screwed up. I'm a horrible person. The three of you have been nothing but kind to me, and I— I—I don't know, went crazy."

"I can't argue with the first part, but you aren't a bad person. You're too close to the situation. Got the rug pulled out from under you, and you're fighting to recover. It's been a long couple of years."

JD met Mitch's kind eyes, fighting back the tears.

"I'm sorry. Can you ever forgive me?"

"Already done, let's sit," he said, pointing toward a wooden bench. Mitch took her hands in his. "The truth is, there's more to the story about Jess and me than the others know."

JD's stomach began to churn. She fought back the panic filling her body.

As if Mitch could read her panic, he continued, "It's not bad. Jess and I had sex several times. It seems we were both trying to figure out who we were. We felt safe with each other. I'm not sure how to explain it. We were great friends, I loved her, and I think she loved me, but not the mad-crazy-can't-live-without-you love."

"Okay," was all JD could whisper.

"We even discussed getting married, having children, but having our own lives. That's what people did then. Especially those from families like mine. My parents knew I was gay but hoped I'd find a woman and settle down, even if the marriage was in name only."

"What happened?"

"I don't know. You know how I explained you were special to Derrick, and he couldn't introduce you to the lifestyle because he couldn't debase you? I couldn't do those things with Jess. I figured she went to Derrick to find out what it was all about. Then she was gone, and I wasn't able to ask. I was mad at Derrick at that time and blamed him."

"Why are you telling me this?" JD asked as the old doubts began to flood in.

"Because, in retrospect, I concluded that Derrick did nothing wrong. Not to mention, if I wanted to screw him over, I could've done it years ago. Johnathan didn't tell you what he knew because there was nothing there but more hurt and anguish."

"So, the three of you discussed it and decided not to tell me?"

"No. He called last night, and we talked. Well, he talked, and I listened. I think him not being here today has more to do with Johnny Walker than what happened at your house. Yes, he was upset because he felt betrayed but guilty for not telling you."

She felt the anger starting to rise. "I'm not a china doll you have to protect," JD said, standing and taking a few steps.

Mitch took her hand. "Come, sit, let me explain. Sweetie, we've all been walking a tightrope about what to tell you. Not because we're hiding things, but because we thought we were going to lose you completely. That's why the three of us were insistent you go away. You were physically and mentally beaten, and we thought you were going to die." This time there were tears in his eyes.

"Mitch, I'm sorry," JD said, leaning into his arms. "I'm confused, hurt, and upset. The trial starting next week has me on edge."

"I know. Do three things for me?"

"Of course."

"One, put on your big-girl panties and buckle up for the trial. You can do it, I know. Second, take Johnathan some chicken soup and fresh bread. Third, come have a glass of wine with me while the kitchen puts together a picnic."

"Thanks, Mitch, you are the best." JD leaned in and kissed him on the mouth. "I love you, you know."

"Oh, you say that now, but wait until I propose, and you have my children."

JD laughed. "Oh, wouldn't that get the gossip mill churning?"

****

JD had a death grip on the basket as she rang the doorbell at Johnathan's house. Her only saving grace was Mitch put the food in a hamper. At least she had something to start the conversation, not begin with begging for forgiveness. He wouldn't answer her calls, so she'd face the lion in his den and get the groveling over before tomorrow morning.

She rang the bell again, waited, nothing, and rang the bell again. What was his problem? She'd start knocking, hell, pounding on the door if she had to. Make a scene, disturb the neighbors. Well, the neighbors weren't that close. She was about to do that when the door opened slightly.

"For Christ's sake, JD, come in out of the blinding light," he said, covering his eyes with his hand. "I never knew my door chime was so damn loud. If it rang again, I was going to shoot it and maybe the person who made me crawl to the door too." He turned, left her standing there, and headed to the living room, and collapsed on the sofa.

JD followed, speechless. Johnathan looked like death warmed over. His eyes were puffy, and well-pronounced dark circles ringed them. He was shoeless and wore sweatpants and a T-shirt, which spoke volumes. "You okay?"

"If you are going to stay, lower your voice, or I may be forced to kill you. No jury would convict me. You come into a man's castle, yelling, oh, never mind. What do you want? This better be damn important. Can't you see I'm dying?" Johnathan said and scrubbed his hands over his face.

"I came to apologize, but I'll get to that. I think you need this more."

He opened his eyes as she waved the basket.

"Tell me that's from Mitch and you have a mason jar of his secret recipe, and all is forgiven."

JD placed the basket on the table and removed a mason jar of a disgusting-looking brownish-red liquid. "Here you go," she said, handing him the container. "I have food, but I'll save that for later. I'll go make coffee." She wasn't sure he heard her. He was laser-focused on the jar.

Johnathan chugged it down and handed JD the jar. "Give me fifteen minutes, and I'll be right as rain or close enough," he said and stomped upstairs. "Then we can talk."

****

JD popped the bread dough in the oven, made herself at home, and set the kitchen table for lunch. She was pouring the soup in a pot when Johnathan, dressed in his normal slacks and button-down shirt, made his way down the stairs. He looked no worse for the evening events.

She handed him a large mug of coffee. "I'm really sorry about last night. I'm just—I don't know what's wrong with me. Can you please forgive me?"

"Of course I can," he said before taking a sip of coffee. "It seems at every turn you are keeping secrets and not coming to us for help. I know you lost sleep over the situation. I also understand how much you love Derrick. What he did to you was wrong on many levels. If I'd had any idea, I'd have stepped in."

Johnathan held up his hands when she started to

speak. "Let's table that for now. There's something more important. I know it's bad to put the negative stuff out there, but I think Derrick is going to be convicted. Are you going to be okay if that happens?"

JD pulled the bread from the oven, placed it on a wooden board, and poured soup into the bowls. She sat, folded her hands in her lap, and stared out the window. "I know, you're right. I asked him about the plea deal. He refused. I think he has sealed his fate."

Her eyes met Johnathan's. "I'll find my way too, with my friends' help," she said, touching his hand.

Chapter Eleven

The trial was like watching a slow-moving train wreck, but JD couldn't stop watching. As promised, she didn't attend any of the proceedings but was glued to the television when court was in session. She, Mitch, Johnathan, and Benjamin had dinner each evening and discussed the day's events.

No one was surprised when the verdict came quickly, nor by the outcome: guilty on all counts. Including first-degree murder, a capital offense in Florida, which meant Derrick had two possible sentences: death, or life without the possibility of parole. She had no doubt which it would be.

****

JD made her way through security She had to see Derrick. She couldn't cry. She had to keep her emotions in check. Be strong for both of them. The knot in her belly grew. It was hard to breathe. Her body began to relax as the Xanax flowed through it. She could do this. She had to do this. She squared her shoulders and entered the attorney-client room.

Johnathan rose when JD entered the room, and he pulled out the chair for her. Derrick sat cuffed and shackled across from her. She slid her fingertips to touch his.

"I'm sorry," she whispered.

"It's not your fault. I didn't kill her, but if I'd

remained faithful to you, I wouldn't be in this situation. I'm the one who should say I'm sorry. You loved me unconditionally, and I took that for granted. Please forgive me," Derrick said, his voice losing power with each word.

JD laid her hands over his. "Of course, you taught me so much; I'm sorry," she said but was unsure it was true. Derrick needed to hear the words.

"There's no touching," the guard barked.

"Sorry," she said, pulling her hands away. Tears burned the back of her eyes.

"I'll see you tomorrow to discuss how to approach the sentencing," Johnathan said.

"Do me a favor, Johnathan. Please take care of JD."

"I don't need anyone to take—" JD began but stopped when Derrick raised his palm.

"Baby, please give me this one. I need to know that you are okay. Please?"

JD scrubbed her hand over her face, sighed, and said, "Okay."

"No problem," Johnathan said. "You ready?" he asked JD.

"I was going to stay a bit longer."

"I want to go back to my cell and rest. Go have dinner. I'll see you tomorrow," Derrick said, more to the guard than his visitors.

The couple made their way out of the jail and into the mob of reporters. Benjamin was waiting for them at the curb.

JD climbed in the backseat and let her head fall back against the seat. No tears would come. She felt numb and lifeless. Mentally, she berated herself for her actions and poor decisions. She clasped her hands in her lap and wondered how things could have been different.

****

JD rushed out the back door of the courthouse. She'd slipped away before the press cornered her. Snowflakes dusted her navy-blue coat. Snow in Tallahassee. What the hell? Traffic buzzed by her on Monroe Street, she felt the wind, but she didn't hear it. She felt like she was walking through a dream, the world rushed by, but she was numb.

Derrick had been sentenced to death, but she felt nothing. No anger, no regret, no fear. Her body was empty. No matter how fast she walked, she couldn't outrun the growing panic.

The cold north wind spread and dried what had been a never-ending flow of tears across her cheeks. How far had she walked? She frantically searched for a sign. She was at the corner of Monroe and Harrison streets: blocks from the office. There were bound to be reporters waiting everywhere.

JD shook her head, trying to pry her brain from the haze. She realized her hands stung from the cold. Gloves, where were her gloves? She found them in her pocket. Slipping them on seemed an impossible task as her fingers shook and ached from the cold.

She momentarily took refuge from the cold wind by stepping beside an old building. She checked her pockets again. No cell. It was in her purse, locked in her office drawer. She discovered a small bag of beef jerky. *What the hell?*

The snowfall was heavier now. Her whole body shook. She'd have to walk back to the office. But it was twenty blocks, if her math was correct, and all uphill.

Perhaps she was having a mental breakdown. It

never snowed in Tallahassee. A thought flashed in her head, *Tallahassee Democrat* headline for tomorrow: "Ex-fiancée of Convicted Killer Found Frozen to Death in Apparent Suicide."

JD heard the small whimper; she followed the faint noise. Her heels caught in the mud as she trudged down the alley.

Without thinking, she climbed on her hands and knees in the mud. Peering under the dumpster, she saw a small ball of silver-and-gray hair.

"Hello, little one," JD said to the mass. "You aren't one of those nutria rats from South America, are you?" Now JD was sure she was having a psychotic episode.

Her hand shook, perhaps from fear or cold, as she offered whatever this thing was, a small piece of beef jerky.

Slowly, a snout appeared from the tangled ball of hair. It was a dachshund. No, it couldn't be. But as the small creature inched toward her, JD was sure it was a wiener dog. The animal might be scared and cold, but hunger was winning out.

Six bites of jerky later, JD sat with the cold, mud-covered dog cradled in her lap. She wrapped the shivering animal in her cashmere scarf. "Well, we are both quite the sight, I bet. We need to find some help. It isn't like this is Siberia."

She struggled through the mud and reached the sidewalk. There was a store within a few feet. She held her head high and limped into the flooring shop on one broken heel. "Here we go, little one. I guess they'll know right away we aren't here to buy carpet."

JD caught her reflection in the mirror before a salesperson reached her. She was caked in mud. She had obviously, at some point, wiped her face. Streaks of blood and dirt covered her face. She knew the dog needed emergency care.

Before the salesperson could speak, JD held up her hand. "I have an emergency and need to use your phone." Bewildered, he handed her his cell. She quickly dialed the only person she could always count on. He answered on the first ring.

"JD, where are you?" Johnathan asked.

****

"I'm sorry about your car," JD said as she paced the emergency vet waiting room.

"No problem," Johnathan replied. "Are you sure you're okay? I can take you home to change. Sandi said it would be a while. They have to run tests."

"Your friend Sandi is the best, right?" was JD's only response as she turned and walked in the other direction.

"Yes. You're going to catch a cold. In case you haven't noticed, you're barefoot, soaking wet, and covered in mud from head to toe."

She waved him off with her left hand. "I washed my face, didn't I? How long has it been?"

"Five minutes since the last time you asked."

JD ran her hands down the front of her jacket and locked eyes with Johnathan. "Look at all the blood. She's so small and thin." She felt her bottom lip start to quiver and the tears overflow.

Johnathan was at her side in seconds and pulled her into his arms. "It will be okay."

JD clung to Johnathan and sobbed. She wasn't sure if he meant the dog or the Derrick situation. It didn't matter. It felt good to be comforted. He held her long after she stopped crying. She rested her head against his shoulder.

"Johnathan." A woman's voice broke the spell. JD stepped back and wiped her face with her hands.

"Yes?" JD asked as a pit of dread hit her stomach.

Sandi took JD's hand and patted it. "She's going to be okay. You found her in time. Let's go to the exam room and talk."

Tears began to flow again. "What's wrong with me?" JD asked Johnathan as the three walked into the brightly decorated room.

"At the risk of being beaten about the head and shoulders, you, my dear, are acting like a typical woman." He held up his hands and whispered, "But I promise, I'll never tell a soul."

JD felt a smile grow on her face. "Thank you."

Sandi flipped on the light box behind the X-rays. "You see this area here?" she asked, pointing to a dark spot about the size of a lemon.

"Yes," JD said, nodding her head.

"It's a pocket of infection. I'll do surgery to clean the area and evaluate the source."

"Okay." There was something in Sandi's tone and mannerisms that said there was more. JD waited for her to continue. Like everything else in her life, she waited for someone else to provide the answer.

"Based on the number tattooed in her ear, I'm sure she was a breeder. The infection is probably from her last litter of puppies. I also suspect she was recently attacked. I'll clean those injuries and treat them as needed."

"What about her back? I know with dachshunds it can be an issue." It was Johnathan who spoke this time.

JD felt a peaceful sensation when Johnathan placed his hand on her lower back.

Sandi slipped another X-ray in place and ran her finger along the print. It seemed to be fine. "JD, I understand you found her. She's not your responsibility. You can leave her with me. I'll take care of her. There isn't a microchip, which isn't a surprise."

"No, I want her! I'll pay the bills. Please don't take her away." Her reaction was way over-the-top, but she couldn't stop her voice from rising.

"That's not what I meant," Sandi said, rounding the exam table and taking JD's hands. "She is yours; I'll begin the surgery as soon as she's stable. You can take her home in a few days."

"I'm sorry. It's been a very unusual day. Can I see her?"

"Sure, this way. Do you have a name?"

"Justice," JD said without a thought.

"I like it," Johnathan said.

Justice lay on a metal table, wrapped in a blanket. A young lady stroked her snout with a small cloth.

"Hello," JD said. "You're going to be fine." Her voice broke, and the tears began. She scratched the small dog between the ears and whispered, "You're going to be okay. We're both going to be okay."

Sandi placed a hand on JD's shoulder. "Here's my prescription for you. Go home, take a hot shower, and eat something. I promise to call immediately if there's a problem. She's a sick little girl, but she'll be fine. You saved her life."

"I think she has saved mine too," JD replied before turning her attention to the dog. "Okay, Justice, I'll be back." She placed her nose to the snout of the dog and whispered, "I love you." The animal opened her eyes. JD was positive she saw a glimmer of hope. "This is going to be a new beginning for both of us."

****

"Here you are," Johnathan said, pulling his car into the garage.

"Thanks for coming to my rescue," JD said, unlocking the door. "I guess I owe you for the extra guards to get through the reporters, and your car is a mess."

"Don't worry. I figured you'd turn up eventually. I was concerned you disappeared after the verdict," Johnathan said, hanging his hat and coat on the rack.

"I thought I was prepared, but based on my running away, wallowing in the mud like a pig, and breaking a heel, I was in my own delusional world. Give me a few minutes to freshen up. Make yourself at home."

"I'm going to use the downstairs bath and clean up." Johnathan held up his gym bag.

"Oh my, I guess I owe you for a suit too. Yours is covered in mud."

"I hope that's all it is," Johnathan said with a chuckle.

JD stopped, leaned against the banister, and fought back tears. "The first person I thought of was you. You're always there for me, no questions asked. You're a true friend. Thank you."

"No problem, that's what friends do. Besides, I needed to replace this suit anyway. So, it's a win-win."

JD climbed the stairs, stripped, and tossed her outfit into the trash bin. The garter belt and stockings followed. She'd never wear them again. What did it matter? She could wear old lady's cotton panties and eighteen-hour bras, no one to impress. She laughed at herself in the mirror and turned on the shower.

****

"It's quite empty," JD said from the landing.

"Your refrigerator is more pitiful than mine," Johnathan said as JD descended the stairs.

JD shrugged her shoulders. "The wine chiller is full, and as for dinner, how about lobster mac and cheese, salad, garlic bread, topped off with pecan pie?"

"Sounds amazing. Not doubting you, but where is it hidden? I've seen inside your refrigerator," Johnathan said, opening the wine.

"Courtesy of Mitch, it'll be here in about thirty minutes." JD grabbed two wine glasses.

"Have I told you lately I love you," he said, pouring the wine. "I'm starving. I couldn't eat this morning," he added quickly.

"I love you too. I don't know what I'd have done without you over the last few years." She walked around the island and leaned against it next to him. "I wish Sandi would call."

"I'm sure Justice will be fine," he said, pausing before continuing. "I'm sorry about Derrick's conviction and sentencing."

JD turned to face him. "Johnathan, there was nothing you could've done. I saw the writing on the wall after the prosecution's never-ending parade of women describing in detail how they'd taken part in BDSM activities. Three testified how they used the safe word several times before he stopped the cutting. It was all too horrific; I knew what the outcome would be. We really had nothing to build a defense on." JD drained her glass and set it on the island.

"I'm still sorry," he said, filling their glasses again. "Is it too early to ask what you will do?"

"Still taking it one day at a time. I'd like to stay at the firm if that's okay."

Johnathan took her in his arms. "No question, no question at all. Hell, the carpet in your office is still fresh," he said and kissed her forehead.

She laid her head on his chest and listened to the smooth sounds of his heartbeat. It supplied a wonderful calm, and it felt good to be held. It had been too long since someone's strong arms held her. At the same time, it was strange to have another man this close. It even felt wrong on some levels.

Why should she feel like this when Derrick had torn her world apart with his lies? Johnathan was a good friend and colleague. He'd never lie to her. But this little voice in the back of her mind drummed home that she'd have bet her life Derrick wouldn't either.

A knock stopped JD's racing mind; dinner had arrived just in time. She needed to get her own house in order and figure out what to do with her life now. Derrick would never get out of prison. It was time for new dreams.

****

Johnathan looked at Benjamin as they waited for Derrick. "We agreed on this?"

"Yes. He's not going to like it, but JD deserves better," Benjamin answered, staring down at the floor. "I figured he'd be convicted but was hoping for a Hail Mary."

Johnathan was about to respond when Derrick was led into the room. None of the men spoke as he shuffled to the table and sat.

"How are you?" Benjamin asked.

Derrick raised one shoulder in response. "Thought

I'd adjust, but death row is, well, death row. Feels like ten years, not ten months."

"We've begun the appeal process," Johnathan said.

"We're still investigating. Whoever set you up had to leave a trail. New DNA techniques are breaking every day," Benjamin said.

Derrick shook his head. "Thanks, I know you're doing everything you can. I understand I won't be leaving anytime soon. How is JD? I hoped she might be with you."

"JD's hard to read. She keeps her cards close to her chest. Justice gives her something to focus on," Johnathan responded.

"I know, she showed me the dog's graduation picture from Canine Good Citizen Class. Just what she needs, a dog to take care of."

As Derrick spoke, Johnathan picked up the hostility in his voice but let it pass as he said, "She has signed her up to be trained as a therapy dog. Justice comes to work with her every day and gives her something positive to focus on. I think it's a good thing."

Benjamin cleared his throat. "Derrick, we're worried about her; she's spiraling again. That's one of the things we wanted to talk to you about."

"I've told her to slow down," Derrick said.

"You need to do more than that," Johnathan said firmly.

"What does that mean?"

Johnathan saw the red flare in his friend's eyes before he spoke. "You need to let her go. Truly free her. Tell her to move on with her life."

"Dammit, I can't do that. Knowing she'll be there when I get out is all that keeps me going."

Benjamin spoke this time. "You and I both know that isn't going to happen, for a long time, if ever. You didn't kill the woman, but you weren't honest about a host of things. You certainly weren't the faithful, loving man you portrayed yourself to be."

"Could you trust someone who lied to you like that? JD needs to build a life. She deserves a husband, children, a family, and happiness. Not tied to you. Is that what you really want?"

"I can't let her go. She's all I have," Derrick said as tears ran down his face.

"What does she have?" Johnathan asked flatly.

"Officer at the door, I want to go back to my cell," Derrick shouted from the table.

****

JD rested her head on the steering wheel and reminded herself to breathe. Her emotions were running rampant. She felt guilty for leaving Justice and panicked at visiting the prison again. The dog loved daycare, and the staff loved Justice. JD had to visit Derrick, no matter her discomfort. She couldn't abandon him, especially at his lowest point.

"Get a grip, girl," she said to her reflection in the mirror, checked her lipstick, and slid out of her new, shiny, red sports car.

Even as an attorney, it took longer to get through security to see a death row inmate. She'd been to Raiford to meet with clients when the firm took over their appeal process. But visiting Derrick was a different matter. Her stomach churned at the thought of him in the small cell twenty-three hours a day.

She hung her suit coat on the chair and paced. She had to be strong for Derrick. She plastered on her best smile when she heard keys clang against the lock. It didn't show, but her stomach dropped at his appearance. Her first impulse was to run to him, but she couldn't do that.

"Hello, Derrick," she said as the officer led him to the table and cuffed him to a bar.

"Hey."

JD heard the forced strain in his voice. Her throat felt like she swallowed dust. "I'd ask how you're doing, but I can tell." She allowed her fingertips to briefly touch his.

"You look good. Jeans the new outfit for work?"

Was that sarcasm she heard? "Thanks, I'm not working today. The firm may be progressive, but denim will never be in."

Derrick slid his hand back. "Thanks for coming, there's something I need you to do for me."

"Anything."

"Move on with your life."

"What?"

"We broke the engagement to reduce your exposure, but not the promise. You need to move on and build a life. I'll probably never get out of here," he said, looking around the small room.

"Don't give up. I've stood by you all this time through everything."

"I know, I'm sorry, but it's different now. I love you and always will, but I've screwed up your life enough."

"But—" JD began, shaking her head.

"Johnathan and Benjamin are handling my case; Mitch is taking care of the money end. You'll never want for anything. I've seen to that. Please go, JD. I'm sorry."

JD picked up her jacket and left the room. She

managed to get to her car before the tears began. She'd known it was coming. It had to. Why did it have to hurt so much? How could she feel regret and relief at the same time? Emotion overload. It had been that way since the first panicked phone call. What was her plan now?

****

Johnathan leaned against the mahogany stair rail, one ankle over the other. The smooth taste of the thirty-year-old scotch he sipped was the furthest thing from his mind.

Front and center in his thoughts was JD. She was the woman he compared all others to. Tonight, she was dressed in a red, sequined, floor-length gown with a slit to more than mid-thigh. It stopped at the point to make a man fantasize about what another inch might reveal. As she walked, he caught a glimpse of the red stiletto heels. She worked the room, smiling, shaking hands, and schmoozing.

"Johnathan, Earth to Johnathan," Benjamin said, slapping his old friend on the shoulder. "Where the hell were you?"

"Watching our partner work the room. She'll have a bundle of new clients on Monday," Johnathan said before sipping his drink. The cool liquid quenched at least one thirst.

"Can't blame them. Who wouldn't rather look across a desk at her than either of us? Not to mention she's made a name for herself as a family law negotiator," Benjamin said, setting his empty glass on the side table.

"She was a hell of a defense litigator; I was worried when she asked to move to another department, but it looks like my concern was a moot point."

"She lost faith in the judicial system after Derrick's conviction."

"She certainly cleaned out Walter Everson in the divorce settlement last week. She went for the throat," Johnathan replied.

"Or someplace slightly lower," Benjamin said with a chuckle and slipped his hands into his pockets.

"There's still a great deal of anger there. Derrick really did a number on her."

"Do you think he killed the woman?" Benjamin asked in a whisper.

Johnathan let the question hang for a minute before saying flatly, "The jury thought so."

"What do you think?"

"It seems the only logical explanation. He loved pushing the envelope. His sexual games must have finally gotten out of control. It escalated to the point where killing was the only thrill left."

"I agree. I don't see how anyone could have set him up," Benjamin said, selecting a glass of wine from a passing waiter.

"The right person with enough inside information could have done it. But we'll probably never know." Johnathan raised his glass to acknowledge Mitch crossing the room toward them.

"Good evening. JD looks incredibly sexy and happy tonight," Mitch said, joining his friends.

"I'm afraid it is all part of her façade. The hurt still runs deep. It's hard to catch her not playing the part she's fashioned to keep people at bay," Johnathan said before taking another sip of the scotch.

"She has no idea how sexy she is. Are you still in love with her?" Mitch asked Johnathan over his glass.

"What?" was all Johnathan could utter.

"You heard him. Answer the question, Counselor," Benjamin teased.

"Let's say I'm biding my time. I have asked her out twice a week for a long time, and she always turns me down."

The men watched JD cross to them. "Well, here are the three most handsome, available bachelors in town." She kissed all three on the cheek and linked arms with Mitch.

"When are you two on the auction block? I may bid on you both," she said to Johnathan and Benjamin.

Benjamin leaned in and whispered in her ear, "Please save me from Madeline Bishop, I beg you."

JD let out a full laugh. "Not to worry, my friend. I have it on good authority you'll go to Valerie Jones, even if it cost a small fortune," she said, straightening his pocket-handkerchief.

"Is there something we should know?" Mitch asked as no one missed Benjamin's face turned bright red.

"Appears there is," Johnathan joked.

"I need a refill," Benjamin said and stepped away without further comment.

"Excuse me, it's time for me to fulfill my MC duties," Mitch said, following Benjamin.

"Cheers, any rumors about me?" Johnathan asked, clinking his glass against JD's.

"You'll have to wait and see," JD said and patted his chest.

"You look beautiful tonight. I love your hair down."

"Thank you. You don't have to pay me compliments. I'm okay," JD said.

"Have I ever lied to you?"

"No."

"Then take the compliment."

"Thank you, and you look quite dapper," JD said with a wink.

"Thanks."

Their conversation was interrupted as Mitch made introductions and began the auction. Both Johnathan and JD laughed as Benjamin was escorted onto the stage. He was bright red as Mitch read his bio. The bidding quickly became a battle between Madeline and Valerie. In the end, it was Valerie who wrote a check for five thousand dollars.

"Okay, handsome, you're up next," JD said and pushed Johnathan toward the stage. She watched, and memories of past auctions flooded her mind.

She fought back the tears, remembering when she'd bid and won Derrick. Their date night had been limos, dinner at the Silver Slipper, and a long night of making love. Then he'd proposed. She looked at the dachshund ring circling her finger. Long gone was the diamond.

Of course, that life had been nothing more than lies and deception. All she was to Derrick was a thing to keep his secret life hidden. She felt the depression and doom slipping in but stopped it dead in its tracks. She stepped out of the shadow and decided it was time to begin her life anew.

"The current bid is three thousand dollars. Come on, ladies, any more bids?"

JD looked at Madeline, the current high bidder, smiled, and said, "Ten thousand dollars."

There was a gasp and then silence through the room. Mitch made one more call. Hearing none, he closed the bidding and congratulated JD.

Johnathan made his way back to her. "Thank you."

"No problem, my gutters need cleaning, and the donation is tax deductible."

Until she broke out into a smile, she realized by the look on his face Johnathan thought she was serious. She took his arm and said, "Come on, my friend, buy me a drink."

Chapter Twelve

Johnathan stared out his office window at the Florida Historical Capital Museum. Fall had come to Tallahassee. The leaves had changed from brilliant green to rust, bronze, and garnet. He put on his jacket and headed to his secretary's desk.

"Glenda, hope you have a great holiday. I'm heading out," he said.

"Thank you, enjoy your vacation."

"I'm sure I will. Go home anytime. Here's a little something for you and your family," he said, handing her an envelope.

Glenda took it. "Thank you. Enjoy the mountains."

"See you on Tuesday."

He headed down the hall to take part in what had become a weekly running joke between him and JD. They would banter, he'd ask her out, and she'd politely decline. He reached her door, stopped, and took in the sight. She had no idea how sexy she was—definitely part of her allure.

She was sitting in the middle of her office floor, law books and files all around her. The black stiletto heels thoughtlessly tossed aside. He watched her toes wiggle to whatever the imaginary music was playing in her head. Which, in turn, made the multicolored dachshunds on her socks appear to dance.

Only she would pull off an Armani suit with colored

print socks. Justice, who'd been sleeping, climbed out of her bed, shook from head to toe, and trotted over to Johnathan. "You know we have online research," he said, scooping up the dog.

JD slid her glasses on top of her head. "I know, but I love the smell and feel of the books."

"Nice socks."

"Thanks," she said, wiggling her feet. "You headed home already?"

"I guess, if you call six o'clock early?"

"Where does the time go?" JD said, looking at her pendant watch.

He watched as she set the book aside, stood, and stretched. "Got plans for the holiday?"

"Is there a holiday?" she answered with a laugh.

"Thanksgiving, you know, comes around each year. Give thanks, eat too much, and watch football."

"Oh, that holiday," she said, placing the books on her desk. "I may have a turkey TV dinner in my freezer. I think my Seminoles and those swamp people are playing football. I'll watch that. What about you?"

Johnathan knew the swamp people comment was a dig because two of his brothers were University of Florida graduates. "I'm headed to the family cabin; snow is in the forecast. Justice would love it, wouldn't you, girl?" he asked, turning the dog to face him.

"There's plenty of room, if you'd like to join me, read and relax. You remember those," he said and spoke to Justice. "Perhaps you could connect with your inner wolf."

The quick decline didn't happen; he watched as she bit her bottom lip. "Okay."

"See you later," he said, turned toward the door,

froze, and turned back. "Wait, did you say 'okay'?"

"I did. Is it a problem? If you were being polite, that's fine," JD said, waving her hand.

"No, come along. I'd love the company."

"Okay, when do we leave?"

"Tomorrow, about nine. We could grab dinner and talk about it."

"Give me ten minutes to organize a bit?" JD asked, gathering up pens, highlighters, and legal pads from the floor.

"Sure, no problem. You and I will sit and watch the blue moon rise," he said to Justice.

"Please, what does that mean?" JD asked, placing the supplies on her desk.

"I've been asking you out for I'm not sure how long, and you finally accept."

"Have to keep you on your toes. Plus, maybe it's time to stir the gossip mill," JD replied with a chuckle.

****

Johnathan wasn't sure what caused him to turn, but he was glad he did. One step at a time, he watched her descend the chalet stairs. First, the pencil-thin heels, then shapely legs that seemed to go on and on. Finally, the bottom hem of a very short, red flared skirt swayed left and right, appeared through the open steps. At the bottom of the stairs, she turned to face him.

The bloodred wraparound dress was breathtaking. Even though no cleavage was in view, the black sequin trim formed an X that outlined her ample breasts. To stop his mouth from dropping open, he took a sip of his wine. "You look amazing."

"Thanks. Is that the tie I gave you for your birthday?"

"Yes. It's the only bow tie I own. Would you like a glass of wine?"

"Sounds wonderful. Where's Justice?" she asked as Johnathan poured wine into a stemmed glass.

"Outside chasing something. I think she's connecting with her inner hunter." As he poured himself a glass, he drank in the look of JD sitting on the barstool.

Her feet were crossed at the ankles. She was a woman of classic beauty. The dimples that came into view when she grinned were present, something he realized he hadn't seen in a while. Her lips were painted red to match her dress, and her hazel eyes sparkled.

A single strand of black pearls circled her neck, and earrings hung like teardrops from her ears. Where her engagement ring had been, a silver dachshund circled her finger. A birthday present from him, he recalled with a smile.

"The only thing my spoiled baby hunts is her food bowl." As if on cue, Justice bounded into the room and headed for her dish. She picked up several pieces, carried them to the living room, dropped them, and ate one chunk at a time.

He handed JD a glass and said, "That's a beautiful necklace."

"Gift from Derrick, what I call guilt jewelry. He was always surprising me with presents after business trips. I guess now I know why. Guilt is a wonderful motivator."

Johnathan laughed. "There're many things I could say, but I think I'll leave it alone."

"Good idea," JD said, raising her glass before sipping from it. "Where are we going for dinner?"

"There's a lodge at Natural Bridge. Live music, dancing, great food, and service that can't be beat."

"Sounds outstanding. I can use a bit of pampering. Plus, I'm starving."

"You're in for a treat. The food's amazing. Growing up, we always ate at the lodge when we came up. I love my mother, but she doesn't know a colander from a saucepan. She's completely lost in the kitchen."

"Must have made family dinner interesting."

"She never learned to cook. She grew up in a home with a full staff, as did I. The difference is I learned from the chef. I'm quite handy in the kitchen, even if I must say so myself," he said, raising his glass.

"Good, I'll put myself in your hands this weekend."

"That's exactly what I had in mind." If she knew what he really wanted to do with his hands, she'd run for the hills. Why did Derrick have such a hold on her, and would she ever let anyone else in? Johnathan finished off his wine and placed his glass in the sink. There was no explaining it. He'd let it go again. "Shall we head out?"

****

"How was your dinner?" Johnathan asked as he placed the cup on its saucer.

"It was amazing. I think the blue cheese-topped filet mignon is the best I've had," she said, holding up a finger. "If you tell Mitch I said so, I'll deny it to the grave," JD said before popping the last piece of a yeast roll in her mouth.

"He'll hear nothing from me," he said, crossing his heart with his finger. "Would you like to dance?"

"I would," JD replied, taking the hand he offered, holding tight, and shifting into his arms when they reached the dance floor. They moved around the dance floor in a slow waltz as the band played "You Look So Good in Love." JD placed her head on his chest as their bodies moved together in delicate and fluid movements.

Couldn't she feel his heart pounding? How could she not know how long he'd loved her? What was stopping him from telling her? *Enjoy the moment,* he reminded himself. *One day, she'll figure it out. Maybe when we're eighty and living in the nursing home.* The thought made him almost laugh out loud.

He escorted her from the dance floor to their table. "Would you like dessert?"

"Why don't we get it to go? I have sweatpants and a sweater calling my name. We can cuddle up on the couch, watch a movie, and pig out."

"Sounds like a plan. How about a slice of cheesecake and another of triple chocolate cake?" Johnathan suggested.

"Both my favorites," JD said before finishing her coffee. "I'll go to the ladies' room and meet you in the lobby. Give me time to look around a bit."

Johnathan rose and helped JD with her wrap. "See you in a few." He sighed as she walked away. What was it about this woman who held him captivated? She haunted his dreams and invaded his thoughts. If only he knew how she felt about him. But JD had mastered the art of keeping her emotions in check. One thing that made her an amazing lawyer.

He could propose and see what she said. He felt the smile grow on his lips at the thought. But if he made a move, he could lose her forever. It was stupid to be this wrapped up over a woman he hadn't even kissed.

The server interrupted his thoughts. He ordered dessert, paid the bill, and boxed up his thoughts and feelings. JD needed balance; her life had been ripped apart already. The last thing she needed was someone else to pull the rug out from under her.

****

JD sat her bowl aside and rubbed her stomach. "I'm stuffed."

"Me too, but isn't that what vacation is about?" Johnathan said, standing and gathering up the dishes.

"I'll straighten the kitchen after I walk Justice," JD said.

"Nope, you're my guest. Would you like a brandy?"

"No. I think we'll hit the hay after the walk. It was a great day, thank you," she said picking up the small dog and heading for the sliding glass door.

"It was my pleasure," Johnathan said, placing the bowls and silverware in the dishwasher.

JD walked around the yard. "You're a good baby. I wish everyone was like you—unconditional love, no secrets. Johnathan's nice, but what could he be hiding? Do I really know anyone? Why can't I trust? What's wrong with me?"

As the small dog ran around the yard, JD let her mind wander back to dancing with Johnathan. It felt good being held. It was one thing she missed. There must be something lacking in her. She was never good enough, no matter what she did. The small voice whispered, *Wait for the other shoe to drop.* Nothing good ever lasted. People let her down or left her holding the bag. She was forever picking up the pieces of someone else's mess.

She jumped when Johnathan touched her shoulder. "I didn't mean to scare you. Penny for your thoughts."

JD turned to face him. "I'm confused."

"Anything I can help you figure out?" he asked, lifting her chin so their eyes met.

"All my life, beginning with my parents, people took advantage and let me down. After years, I let my walls down, and Derrick threw our lives and dreams away for one night." She stepped back, held up her hands, and felt the tears flowing down her cheeks. "I know there were many nights, but for me, that's the one that counts. What the hell is wrong with me? Why can't I be enough? Why can't someone love me for who I am?"

Johnathan wrapped her in his arms. "Go ahead, cry, let it out. I'm here. I've got you. We are friends who don't judge." He placed a kiss on her forehead and held tight.

JD held on and sobbed. Her stomach churned, and her head began to pound. "Johnathan, I—" She paused, stepped back, and looked into his eyes. "—I really do care for you. I think if I had the ability to love anyone, it would be you. Part of me died the night of the murder."

"It's okay. I'm not going anywhere. Think of me as your best friend for now."

JD placed her head on his shoulder and whispered, "Maybe I need more time." Oh, how she wished that were true.

****

JD woke feeling like a weight had been lifted. She headed downstairs in pajamas, a robe, and thick woolly socks. The smell of fresh-brewed coffee seemed to drift across the room. She poured a cup of coffee and headed to the deck. The cold air caused her skin to tingle.

She turned in a circle and took in a deep breath. The air was exhilarating. She caught sight of Johnathan striding up the hill. When he was within range, she waved and said, "Good morning, you're up and out early."

"I was up with the sun, full of energy."

"Well, as you see, I slept in," she said, slipping her hands into her pockets.

"Glad to see it, but you better get inside before you catch a cold. It's quite brisk out this morning."

"Let's have coffee and make a plan for the day. I feel, I'm not quite sure, rejuvenated. I guess. Maybe I turned a corner last night." JD took his hand and led him toward the house. "Thanks for being my friend no matter what."

Johnathan turned JD to face him and placed his hands on her shoulders. "I promise you, no matter what, I'll always be here for you. I care for you on many levels. If what you need is a friend, my sweet, here I am," he said and placed a kiss on her forehead and closed her in a hug.

How could she tell him what she wanted? What she craved was her master's firm hand on her ass, driving her toward total surrender and a sexual release beyond anything she had imagined. Johnathan would think she was like Derrick and had lied. He'd question everything she'd said before and after. She had lied through omission, but it was still a lie.

Chapter Thirteen

JD used her key to unlock Johnathan's front door. "It's me; I brought dinner," she shouted, heading toward the kitchen.

"You know where I am," Johnathan bellowed from the bedroom.

She placed the bags on the counter and headed to the back of the house. "Hey, boss," she said from the doorway.

"Hey. I thought Glenda was bringing dinner?" he barked.

"Apparently, after the way you spoke to her at lunch, you're lucky to still have an assistant. It took Benjamin and me all afternoon to convince her not to quit."

Johnathan huffed, frowned, shifted in the bed, but didn't answer.

"I told her you were angry at yourself and in a great deal of pain. You didn't mean to be an unappreciative, nasty son of a bitch," JD said, sitting on the side of the bed.

This time he crossed his arms on his chest. "I'm not; I wasn't. Okay, maybe I was angry. I guess I should apologize?"

JD chuckled and smirked. "Probably better to wait until you can somewhat sound like you mean it."

"Women," Johnathan began.

JD cocked her head and raised an eyebrow.

He placed his index finger on her lips and forced a

smile before continuing. "Please tell me you brought something other than salad. I'm sick to death of vegetables."

"How do a rib eye steak, baked potato, and asparagus sound?" JD asked, leaning over to remove her heels.

"I may be in love. You want to get married?"

"Sure, we can run away. I understand the snow is great in Aspen. Wait, that's what got you into this situation: skiing and injuring your knee, I'll pass."

"I knew there was a reason I kept you around, comic relief," Johnathan said as he shifted toward the side of the bed. "If we aren't running away, I'll settle for a shower."

JD stood and offered her arm. "We can make that happen."

"Thanks," Johnathan said, steadying himself against her as he reached for his crutches.

"You okay?" JD asked. His musky scent made her dizzy. She wanted to push him on the bed and show him how much she wanted him. But it wasn't right. She still craved her mystery man. Johnathan wasn't a stand-in.

"I'm good, just dizzy for a minute."

"Okay?" she asked, stepping back.

"I'm good. The maid left clothes in the bathroom."

"Yell if you need anything," JD said, turning to leave the room.

"JD?"

Her heart stopped at his voice, and she turned. "Would you mind getting a blanket from upstairs. There's a blue one in my bedroom closet. No rush, before you go."

"Sure."

JD needed to regain her perspective. Johnathan wasn't for her. He deserved someone who would give themselves completely. Derrick had killed that part of her. She fought back the tears, and the realization hit her square between the eyes. She was like Derrick now: addicted to the lifestyle. She needed more than a fling. She desired and craved a master.

She couldn't come out to Johnathan. He'd think she'd been into the life all along and had lied about it. Maybe it was time to email the man who haunted her dreams, tell him the whole truth, and see where it would lead. They'd bantered back and forth via email for months, but they both seemed to skirt meeting. Perhaps she should push.

JD forced her hands to work as she washed, buttered, salted the potatoes, and placed them in the convection oven. Thoughts trampled her mind. She'd loved Derrick with all her heart, and look where that had gotten her. Most days, she still struggled to figure which way was up. Like many things, she had accepted this was her new life. She'd be fine by herself.

It was the right thing, she told herself, placing a cast-iron skillet in the oven to heat, and unwrapped and seasoned the steaks.

****

Johnathan covered the bandage over his left knee with plastic and secured it with medical tape. He faced the mirror, ran his fingers over his beard, and asked the reflection, "What the hell are you doing? Haven't you had enough sweaty dreams over her?"

For years, he and JD had danced around each other. What was holding her back? They seemed to be at a crossroads in the mountains, but they were still clearly stuck in the friend zone. He shaved and hobbled into the shower.

How amazing it must be to have someone love you so deeply? Derrick had been a fool and had broken her heart. JD may never be ready to move forward.

The hot water soothed his aching body. He adjusted the shower and sat on the tile bench. His knee ached, but his body craved JD.

His erection was instantaneous and throbbed as he fondled himself. How many times had he pleasured himself thinking of JD? Way too many to count. He closed his eyes and let the fantasy take him. The woman was half JD and half the Mistress from the gala. The two women became one and danced through his mind as he stroked faster and faster. But it was JD's hands that caressed his body, and the voice which drove his passion. He rubbed his balls with his left hand as the release came to his taut body.

His body shook as he hobbled from the shower, dried, and dressed. He had to talk to JD. Tell her how he felt. Tell her everything. That was the rub, wasn't it? He'd have to confess his need to spank her. She'd think he was like Derrick and wouldn't believe he hadn't lied, but hadn't he, by omission? But he'd take the chance. He loved JD. She'd understand. He'd make her understand. As soon as he was up and around. He'd ask her to marry him and give up the spanking.

****

JD turned the potatoes and poured two glasses of white wine before heading upstairs to find the blanket. She'd been to the house multiple times but never his bedroom. It felt like an invasion of privacy. She smiled, opening the door; the space suited him.

A simple, antique bed she knew had belonged to his father, deep earth tone drapes and pillows, and the recovered overstuffed chair they'd found at a flea market faced the window to the backyard. Hardwood floors shined to a high polish. The room smelled like pipe tobacco and scotch. She smiled, thinking she'd tease him because he obviously hadn't given up the pipe after all.

She moved to the walk-in closet and ran her fingers along the suits, shirts, ties, to the casual clothing. She'd seen him in most of them, more so since the incident with Derrick; he'd watched over her for years.

JD took a deep breath and spoke to the ceiling, "Get a grip, girl. It's a man's bedroom, not the Smithsonian."

There was the blanket on the shelf. Of course, he'd be as organized here as at the office. She looked for a stool but didn't see one. In the end, she tugged at the folded fabric. Down came the blanket and a box. She managed to catch the decorative cardboard square as the lid fell to the floor.

JD stared into the box with disbelief. It was a mask; it was *the* mask. Her legs felt weak, and she collapsed to the floor. Thoughts sped through her mind. Johnathan couldn't have been the man at the gala. The man who had pleased her like no other and left her bottom sore for days. She shook her head; it couldn't be. Fearing her wobbly legs wouldn't hold her, she remained on the floor.

She picked up the mask and caressed it. She wound the black ribbon ties around her fingers. No, no, it couldn't be. There had to be masks that were alike. JD removed a black scarf from the box. Under it was the final clue. She retrieved a white business card, a single line of print. An email address. The one she'd been sending messages to for months.

Johnathan *was* the man at the gala. So, they both had secrets.

JD forced herself to breathe. She'd have to get through dinner and decide what to do. *Dinner, shit,* the cast-iron skillet would be way too hot by now. She shoved the box back on the shelf and raced out of the closet.

Halfway down the stairs, she remembered the blanket. She retraced her steps, grabbed the blanket, and took one more look at the box.

"I took the skillet out of the oven. You okay? You look like you've seen a ghost," Johnathan said as she entered the kitchen.

"I didn't know your house was haunted. You should've warned me," JD said, brushing past him into the downstairs bedroom. She tossed the blanket on the bed, let out a slow deep breath, and returned to the kitchen.

"You sure you're all right?" Johnathan asked again as she placed the steaks in the skillet.

"I'm good, tired, long day at the office with one of the partners out playing sick," she teased.

JD's stomach churned as she fought to find the smooth rhythm of their friendship. But everything had changed. Was Johnathan into more than spanking? How much was he like Derrick? Why hadn't he told her? Her mind was swimming. Time seemed to crawl by as they ate. Visions of Johnathan spanking her kept invading her thoughts.

Johnathan placed his hand over hers. "What's up? Your hand was shaking."

JD played with her napkin and forced a smile. "I'm

fine. Everything catching up, I guess."

She chatted away about things at the office while she cleaned the kitchen. Johnathan sat and responded in kind. "You need to get your knee elevated, back to bed with you," JD said, handing Johnathan his crutches.

She was glad he took the crutches and turned before the blush rushed from her toes to the top of her head. She wanted his hands on her. More specifically, she wanted his hand flat on her ass.

She unfolded the blanket and spread it over him. "I'll bring the files you asked about tomorrow. Rest well," JD said, placing a glass of water on the nightstand.

JD was at the bedroom door when he spoke. "JD." Her name seemed to float off his lips.

"Yes?" she responded, turning.

"Drive careful. It's supposed to rain tonight."

"Okay," she replied but didn't leave. "You all right?"

"Yep. Stayed up too long. Thanks for dinner and the company."

"No problem." JD was sure there was something else he wanted to say but chalked it up to her heightened state.

She raced home and opened her computer and typed in the web address, entered her code and email address, took a deep breath, and began to pin her message:

Dearest M,

As I provided before, things in my life appear to be forever complicated. With that said, if I might be so bold as to suggest, I'd like to meet. It is my wish to speak in person. I hope you will grant me this request. Know I'll keep your secret as I know you will mine. If you have doubts, please check with our mutual acquaintance. It's time for me to trust again. I hope you will be my beginning.

Forever your submissive, L

JD read the email over and over, hit Send, and headed to the kitchen for more wine.

****

Johnathan couldn't get comfortable. He shifted the pillows under his knee and took a pain pill. He lay for minutes staring at the ceiling, shifting, thoughts of JD causing great discomfort. "Boy, you are in a mess, aren't you?" he said to the ceiling fan.

Work, he'd work. He laughed and clapped his hands; the light came on. A gag gift from JD. He loved it but would never admit it to her. He read the same lines of the trial transcript over and over. He tossed the file aside and picked up his computer. He'd email his Lisa and let her know this would be his last message. Tomorrow, he'd tell JD how he felt.

It would mark the beginning to his new life. He logged into the VPN and began his message, but a ding announced an incoming email. What would his princess have to say?

He read the email several times and let his head fall back on the pillow. Damn fate. "What the fuck?" He could meet her, see if there was a connection. "No!" he shouted at the ceiling. JD was his future.

His palm itched to feel Lisa's flesh under his hand and see the face behind the mask, but that wouldn't be fair to either of them. He began his response:

Dear L,

I'm not sure who said timing is everything. In this case, it is true. I logged into my account tonight to send you one last message. There is someone in my life, but she is not into the lifestyle. Tonight, I realized she's what I want and need. So much so, I'm willing to walk away from this part of my life. I'll always remember our night together. Please continue to look for the person who can be what you need. If things were only different.

Always, M.

Johnathan stared at the response and decided he'd reach out to Mitch in a few days to ensure their mutual friend was okay. With that thought, he hit Send.

****

JD chugged her wine. What the hell had she done? What if she was wrong? What if Johnathan had been storing the stuff for a friend? As she poured another glass of wine, her computer chimed. A response already? Her heart pounded in her chest, and her hand shook as she hit *Open.* She read the email three times.

There was someone in his life. Well, she'd put an end to that and right now. He was hers. She shut down her computer and rushed upstairs.

****

Johnathan heard the front door open. Benjamin had come by after all, and he needed the distraction. "I'm in the bedroom. I hope you brought ice cream." He listened to the unmistakable sound of ice-pick heels clicking on the hardwood floor.

He raised an eyebrow—certainly not Benjamin, maybe a robber. He laughed and shook his head; no thief would have a key or wear heels. Panic surged through him as Mistress Lisa stepped into view and leaned against the doorframe. "So, you met someone?" Her southern accent was sweet as honey.

She loosened the ties of the ebony cape, and it fell into a puddle of expensive fabric at her feet.

Johnathan's cock sprang to attention, and his heart pounded as the black floor-length lace dress that showed nothing and everything came into view. At lightning speed, his mind returned to the encounter at the gala. He knew all too well what delights were hidden just above the front slit. He enjoyed the journey up the dress to the ample breasts, ending at the black mask.

"What are you doing here? How did you find me? You can't be here." His words seemed to tumble out as panic overtook the sexual desire.

She laughed, walked toward the bed, and turned in a slow circle. "Appears I am."

Johnathan was speechless. He licked his lips. "Mistress, you can't stay. What if someone finds you here?"

"I think it's worth the risk, and I think you will too," the lady said as she stepped closer to the bed. "Perhaps after we talk, you'll realize *we* can have the best of both worlds."

It was a dream, was all Johnathan could think. The combination of pain pills and wine. He was back in the fantasy. The woman's smile was devilish. She slowly licked her lips, wetting the bright-red lipstick. It was like slow motion as she pulled the black ribbon holding her mask in place. If this was a dream, he didn't want to wake up.

With her left hand, the vision removed the mask. "Surprise," JD said.

"Wait, *you're* Lisa? You were at the gala? I—"

JD placed her gloved finger on his lips. "Mitch thought if I went to the gala, I might better understand the lifestyle and Derrick's obsession. May I sit down?"

His mind raced, but the thoughts seemed to freeze.

He tried to speak, but the words wouldn't come out. Finally, he managed one word. "Sure."

JD sat and crossed her legs. Johnathan's mind continued to spin as he stared at the toned, tanned legs.

"I guess I should explain," JD said as she stroked his thigh with her fingertips.

"Okay."

"When I went upstairs to retrieve the blanket earlier, a box fell off the shelf. I found your mask and the cards."

"Okay," Johnathan stammered. Why wouldn't his mouth work?

"So, I guess the question is, shall we talk about this tonight or tomorrow?" JD asked, leaning in so her words caressed his lips.

"Tonight, tomorrow, beautiful, either works with me," Johnathan said as he slipped his hand behind JD's neck and gently urged her lips to his.

****

JD was cold. She felt for the blanket and discovered she wasn't alone. For a split second, fear raced through her, but then the night's events came flooding back. She stretched like a cat and rolled over.

Johnathan's warm smile met hers. "Good morning," he said, caressing her neck and running his fingers through her hair.

"Good morning, yourself." She ran her fingers over the stubble of his beard. Crawled closer and whispered in his ear, "Are we okay?" She didn't want to see the disappointment on his face if they weren't.

Johnathan lifted her chin. "I'm outstanding, and you?"

"Wonderful, absolutely wonderful."

"Come closer, put your head right here," he said,

pointing to his shoulder.

She rested her head on his shoulder, and he pulled her closer. "This is perfect."

"I'm sorry," JD began.

"Are you sorry about last night?"

"No. Before."

"Look at me." When she did, he continued, "We talked everything through last night. Both of us were silly not to have made a move. As you said, it's a win-win. I wish Mitch had said something sooner, but here we are. Where's Justice?"

"Mitch took her home. I'm sure she's having fun with Lewis and Clark. I'll call him later about picking her up."

"There is one thing I'm disappointed about," Johnathan said, playing with her curls.

"What's that?" JD asked.

"I wasn't able to do all things to you I've dreamed about. Seems like you did most of the work last night. Wait until my knee heals."

JD let out a laugh. "I'm not sure I can handle it." She leaned in and kissed his cheek. "But I'll suffer through the best I can."

"That's my girl," Johnathan said, lowering his mouth to JD's.

Chapter Fourteen

JD held tight to Johnathan's hand and took a deep, cleansing breath; her heart was pounding as they entered the Corner Table. What would Benjamin and Mitch think about them as a couple? Sunday brunch was a tradition the four men began in college and continued as they found their chosen field. It had become the perfect kickoff for her week.

Would it seem awkward? Would they accept the couple? JD smiled at the sight of Valerie sitting next to Benjamin, hands joined on the tabletop. She felt the tension drain from her body. This was going to be fine.

"Hey, Valerie, Benjamin," both Johnathan and JD said. JD could read the same uneasiness she felt in the hall in her friend. Seemed this was a day for more than one new beginning. She walked to the woman and gathered her in her arms, and whispered, "I'm glad you're here."

"Thanks. I wasn't sure if I'd fit in. You've been a member of the group for a long time," Valerie said.

JD stepped back. "I felt the same way the first few times," JD said and turned as Mitch entered the room.

"Good morning," Mitch said from the sideboard. "Brunch will be served in about fifteen minutes. What would you like to drink?"

"Coffee and Bloody Mary, please, the one with shrimp and bacon," JD said.

"Good morning, Mitch. Same for me," Johnathan said.

"They'll be out in a flash," Mitch said. "Benjamin, would you and Valerie like another round?"

"Yes, please," Benjamin said.

Johnathan and JD sat at the table across from the other couple. "Valerie, how are things coming with Springtime Tallahassee?"

"It's on track. Something always goes wrong at the last minute. I'm moving forward and will handle damage control when needed," Valerie said.

"I'll be at the meeting next week, find something I can do to help," JD said.

"Excuse me," a waiter said and placed drinks around the table.

Mitch sat at the head of the table. "First, welcome to our newest member, Valerie. I look forward to many happy Sundays in your company, cheers," he said and raised his glass.

"It also appears another couple in our midst has finally come to their senses." He looked to Johnathan and JD and raised his glass. "Cheers," he said.

"Cheers," the group said, raising their glasses.

As the group chatted, food was delivered to the sideboard. "Let's eat," Mitch said as the last waiter left the room.

"This is amazing," Valerie said, adding mixed berries to her already-overflowing plate. "I have to do extra yoga this week."

"I know," JD said, selecting a Belgian waffle, adding berries and cream. "This is my weekly transgression, well, one of them," she added with a laugh.

Mitch stopped JD as she returned to the table. "So, I guess you and Johnathan finally figured it out?" he said with a wink.

"You knew all along, didn't you?" JD asked.

"Yes," he said after sipping his coffee.

"Why didn't you tell us?"

"You two had to figure it out. Johnathan has loved you for years. You needed to be ready." He took her plate and sat it on the table. Then took her in his arms. "You're well suited for each other. I couldn't be happier."

"Me either," Benjamin said, patting JD on the back. "Thank you both."

"How about me?" Johnathan asked.

Benjamin turned and said, "It certainly took you long enough."

They all laughed and headed to their places at the table.

JD sipped her drink and smiled. Her life was turning out the way it should. Life with Johnathan would be exciting. They'd marry, have children, and a wonderful life together. Everything in the past was boxed away. She turned her attention to the friendly conversation around the table and the wonderful food. All was as it should be.

****

Johnathan and JD strolled hand in hand through MacClay Gardens. Fall had arrived with all its glorious colors. Johnathan carried the picnic basket filled with Mitch's wonderful cooking and bottle of champagne Justice followed behind, enjoying her sniffafari.

"I love this time of year. My parents brought us here for picnics when my brothers and I were growing up. It was their special place," Johnathan said and fought back the growing tension in his stomach. His father had proposed here. He planned to do the same. It would be their special place too. They would bring their children here to play and learn about love.

Johnathan spread the red plaid blanket under an oak tree and placed the basket to one side

"It's beautiful," JD said, stopping at the water's edge.

"Yes, it is," Johnathan said, slowly turning JD to meet his gaze. He leaned in and gently touched his lips to hers. "JD, I love you."

She ran her hands around his neck. "I love you too, Johnathan," she said and returned his kiss, using her tongue to dance with his and deepen the kiss.

"You're so beautiful and drive me absolutely crazy," Johnathan said, stepped back, took a knee, pulled a box from his jeans pocket, opened it, and took her hand. "Jennifer Dianne Ellis, would you marry me?" Johnathan had worried over the ring choice for weeks; it was far from the large diamond Derrick had given her.

JD looked at the square-cut diamond set in a simple band. "Yes, Johnathan, yes."

"The ring was my great-grandmother's. Do you like it?" he said, sliding it on her finger.

"Johnathan, it suits me to a tee. I love it!" she said, holding it up so they could see it shine in the sunlight. "You know me so well. I love you, Johnathan."

He brushed her cheek with his palm, folded her in his arms, and whispered, "You'll be mine forever, JD, always my equal, sometimes my wife, and sometimes as my submissive. You okay with that?"

"Yes, Master," she whispered into the crook of his neck.

Johnathan swatted JD lightly on the butt. "Let's

have lunch, enjoy the gardens a bit more, and head home. I have another appetite for you to satisfy."

"Your wish is my command," JD said, sitting on the blanket.

Johnathan began unpacking the gourmet meal. He could always count on Mitch. Everything was always perfect.

****

JD sat, paced, and sat again. She knew it was the right thing. Derrick needed to hear the news from her. She hid the shock when she saw him. He was thin and drawn. "Hi," she said.

"Hey."

As they sat across from each other, JD's thoughts drifted back over the years to a time she loved him more than herself. When all she wanted was to be his wife, have their children, and grow old together. Would've done anything he asked. Only he didn't share or tell her about the most important thing to him. Neither spoke as tears ran down her face. She closed her eyes and fought back the tears, opened them, and met his cold stare.

"Why did you come, JD?"

"I wanted you to hear it from me." JD shuffled in her chair and swallowed down dread in her throat. "I'm getting married."

He lowered his head and didn't speak for minutes. When their eyes met again, JD could tell the words were forced but also read controlled rage.

"You deserve to be happy."

She knew him well enough to read the emotions in his eyes, but sat in silence.

"Tell me, who's the lucky man?"

"Johnathan," she said, watching as he balled his fist.

"He has good taste and has always had a thing for you. How long have you been dating?" Before she could answer, he added, "Since I was locked up?" The words were thick with sarcasm.

"Really? That's how you want to spin this? We've been seeing each other for a few months. You know we've always been friends. I'm not sure exactly where it changed. You were the one who insisted I move on with my life."

His response was a stare. "So I did," he said, leaning back in the chair.

The anger she thought was gone flowed out like a volcano. She stood and stared down at him. "We had everything, or at least I thought we did. You were the one who lied, cheated, and didn't give our relationship a chance. If you'd only trusted me." JD held up her hands, closed her eyes, and took a deep breath. But the anger didn't pass.

"You were the one who hid a major part of your life and put yourself in this situation," she said, turning in a circle in the small room. "What am I supposed to do, visit you here every week and not have a life? This isn't a simple misunderstanding, you selfish bastard." JD pointed her finger. "You, you did this to yourself.

"If you think Johnathan was anything other than a gentleman until I was ready to find love again, then you must not know him any better than I know you. Stupid me. I thought you would be happy for me. Once again, I thought about your feelings. Came here to tell you about this, and I should have known you would make this all about you." JD grabbed her jacket and headed to the door.

Derrick waved his handcuffed hands. "Wait, I'm

sorry. It's a shock, and you are right; I am a bastard. Please stay awhile. I've missed our talks. Tell me about your practice."

Her anger still bubbling, she sat. Damn, what was it about this man? He still pulled her in. "I'm still practicing family law. You know I went back to school, and I'm now a licensed mental health counselor. I hold weekly sessions for couples who think they want to divorce." She drew invisible circles on the metal table as she spoke.

"I bet you're great at it. You enjoy it?" he asked, leaning back in the chair.

"I've got a pretty good success rate when both people give it their best. I still spend plenty of time in court, but I think I've found my niche." She leaned in a bit and whispered, "You're still the only one who knew my ultimate goal."

Derrick smiled, but it didn't reach his eyes. "To be a judge. I have no doubt you'll make it. Nothing can stop you once you set your mind to it." His face turned sullen. "I'm really sorry for the pain. You didn't deserve it. Seems like you're back on track. Go now, JD, be happy, don't look back."

JD brushed her hand over his. "Goodbye, Derrick." She did what he asked, walked from the room, and fought the urge to look back. Like everything else, she'd leave this behind and move forward. That didn't stop the tears when JD reached her car.

Chapter Fifteen

The sheer curtains danced in the breeze through the two sets of French doors of the Victorian-style bedroom. The air carried the smells of summer: honeysuckle, roses, and magnolia. JD couldn't have asked for a more perfect wedding day.

JD turned in the trifold mirror as before. Gone was the black dress and mask. In its place, she wore a shimmering ballgown and cathedral train. The illusion bodice and back set off the design. She turned from side to side, making the sequins and sparkle tulle cast small prisms of light across the wooden floor.

Gone was the mermaid-style gown as well as the over-the-top pomp and circumstance Derrick had insisted on. A knock at the door stopped her from heading down a painful rabbit hole.

"Come in," she said.

Mitch strolled into the room, carrying her bouquet. The cascading multicolored bouquet was filled with purple, teal, and white flowers and succulents. Mid-center was a black orchid and one peacock feather. "I thought you'd like a little reminder of the night that brought you together." His grin was infectious.

"Just can't help yourself, can you? It's lovely. Thank you for hosting the wedding," JD said, placing the bouquet on the table. "How's my groom?"

"He loved the cuff links and asked me to deliver

this." Mitch handed her a square navy-blue box. Tears stained the back of her eyes as she caressed the silver necklace. At the end were three rings, one circled in diamonds, the second rose gold, and the third yellow gold. It was harder to keep the tears in check as she read the note.

My love, this infinity necklace symbolizes eternity, empowerment, and my everlasting love. I'll be waiting for you at the altar. Today you are giving me the most precious gift: becoming my wife.

"Oh my, the dress is amazing," Valerie said, entering the room. "Simply breathtaking." She stepped to JD and handed her a glass of champagne. "Drink up. The photographer's about finished with the guys; he'll be up soon."

"Cheers," she said and clinked glasses with both her companions. "Now my gifts, Valerie," she said, handing her a small gift bag.

"JD, it's perfect," she said, holding out the emerald brooch for Mitch to see.

"Let me pin it on. It goes perfectly with your dress," Mitch said, stepping back.

"I love it, thank you," Valerie said.

"I had a little help from Benjamin and Mitch," JD said, picking up a box and handing it to Mitch. "What to give a man who has everything?" JD touched her lips, smiled, and handed Mitch a box.

He unwrapped it and burst into laughter. "Why my very own Billy Big Mouth Bass?" He removed the fish and pressed the button; the plaque-mounted fish's mouth began to sing "Take Me to the River."

JD began laughing too. She read the shock on Valerie's face, which caused her to laugh even harder.

"Wait, wait." She held up her hands. "The guys and I always do gag gifts; sorry, I should've warned you."

"Okay, I was wondering if I missed a memo," Valerie said and finished her glass of champagne.

"Okay, last-minute check. Your something old is the handkerchief from my mom, the something new, obviously the necklace, something borrowed is the brooch on the ribbon of your bouquet," Mitch said, circling back to JD.

"Valerie, the brooch belonged to Johnathan's great-great-grandmother. It has been worn by brides for generations."

"Oh my," Valerie said, picking up the flowers. "What a beautiful profile cameo."

"Martha, Johnathan's mom, said it's a honey-colored semitransparent hard stone," JD said, slipping the matching earrings into place. "These are reproductions Johnathan's father had made for Martha."

"How about the something blue?" Valerie asked, pouring another round of drinks.

"That's well hidden for my groom to find." JD raised the hem of her dress to reveal a blue lace garter.

"We have them all except a sixpence for your shoe," Mitch said, reaching into his pocket. "I know it is generally the father of the bride who provides this, but I took the liberty of doing the honors," he said, dropping the coin into her left shoe.

JD bit her quivering lip, stepped to Mitch, and let the tears come.

"All right now, I know what we need." Mitch patted JD on the back before hitting the button on the robotic bass mounted on the wall. The tail began to whish as he belted out a happy tune.

JD dabbed her eyes, touched up her makeup, and said, "Where's the photographer? I'm ready to get married."

****

Johnathan couldn't stand still. He shuffled his feet, ran his hand over his beard, kept looking down the aisle and at the attendees, and back again. His senses were on overload. The fountain flowing into the fish pond sounded like a tsunami, and the air was thick with mint, thyme, and rosemary planted on the path near the seats.

Benjamin placed his hand on Johnathan's shoulder and spoke softly, "You seem pretty anxious to be linked to a ball and chain."

Johnathan grinned and looked over his shoulder. "I never thought I'd marry, especially to JD."

"No other woman had a chance; you and I both know it."

The men turned when the music shifted. Johnathan heard Benjamin let out a low "Wow" when Valerie stepped into the opening of the garden. He had to admit she was drop-dead gorgeous in the off-the-shoulder eggplant dress. Dangling emerald earrings, bracelet, and brooch set off the purple gown.

Johnathan turned to his friend and whispered, "You'd be a fool to let her get away. Beautiful, smart, and she laughs at your jokes." He could tell his friend was already toast. The thought caught in his throat. The first bars of the wedding march sounded, and JD appeared at the garden entrance with Mitch and Justice in a white dress and bow.

Johnathan was spellbound. His heart raced, he felt his knees buckle and his body tremble. The sight of the gorgeous creature walking toward him took his breath away. He locked eyes with the woman he loved. She was a vision in white. Her smile was contagious. They gazed at each other until she reached him. If he'd had any doubts, they melted at that moment.

Mitch lifted JD's veil, kissed her cheek, and placed her hand in Johnathan's. With her touch, everything was instantly right.

Johnathan mouthed the words, "I love you."

JD lowered her eyes slightly, leaned in, and whispered, "Do you approve, Master?"

His wink answered her question.

Mitch moved under the gazebo and faced the couple. "Welcome, everyone who's here to share in this important moment in the lives of Jennifer and Johnathan. To celebrate, acknowledge, and honor the vows they make today by attending, you witness and affirm the truth of their love and commitment to one another. For me, I say it's about time."

Johnathan found it hard to concentrate as Mitch read a passage from the Bible and prayed. He wanted to pull JD into his arms and never let go.

"Johnathan," JD whispered.

He was pulled back to reality by a laugh from the attendees. "What?" he said a bit too loud.

"Vows, Johnathan, the vows," JD whispered with a giggle.

Benjamin laughed, patted Johnathan on the back, and said, "See, she's already having to tell him what to do." By the time the laughing died down, Johnathan was focused.

He took JD's hand and squeezed it slightly. "JD, I love you with every fiber of my being. I promise to love you for the person you are and will become. I promise to nurture and achieve your dreams. I promise to hire a professional, even if I really want to fix something—and would probably make it worse—myself. I vow to take your hand when it's too dark and take Justice out when it's too early. I promise to show you every day how deeply I care for you. Together, we can meet any challenge that confronts us. I pledge myself to you all the days of my life."

****

JD smiled up at Johnathan. Butterflies filled her stomach as she took a deep breath and began. "Johnathan, you were my friend and confidant for years, and I still recall the night I realized you were the man I loved with all my heart. I promise to be your friend, partner, and wife wherever life's adventures take us. I trust, cherish, appreciate, and respect you. Today, I say I do, but I also say I will be by your side in good times and bad. You make me laugh, you challenge me, but most of all, you make me happy. My darling, you are my everything. Today, I give myself to you for the rest of my life."

"The couple will be exchanging rings," Mitch said.

Benjamin handed Johnathan the gold band. "I give you this ring as a symbol of my love and faithfulness," Johnathan said, sliding the ring on JD's finger. "Today, I ask you to wear it as a reminder of the words we've spoken and as a remembrance of my constant love for you."

JD smiled up at her groom, turned to Valerie, and took a matching band. "Johnathan, today I ask you to wear this ring as a reminder of the words exchanged and as a promise I will serve and honor you for the rest of my life," she said, slipping the ring on his finger.

"Now, by the power given to me by the great State of Florida, I now pronounce you husband and wife. Johnathan, you may kiss your bride."

He slid one hand behind JD's neck, and the other ringed her waist and gently pulled her into his arms. He nuzzled her ear and whispered, "Kiss me, my wife."

His brazen eyes met hers. JD stood on her tiptoes, met his passion with her own, her tongue danced with his, and she assaulted his mouth with hers. His hand played in her hair. *This is magic* flashed into her mind. *This is the way it should be.*

"Don't make me get a bucket of cold water," Mitch said, breaking the moment.

Johnathan placed his forehead on hers and murmured, "You are going to be the death of me; I love you."

"Ladies and gentlemen, may I present for the first time, Mr. and Mrs. Johnathan Howe, III," Mitch said as the couple turned toward the crowd.

Johnathan took his bride's hand and headed toward the reception room. JD said, "I wish we could go upstairs before all the festivities; I need to make love to my husband."

"All in good time, my love, all in good time," Johnathan said, swatting her bottom.

Chapter Sixteen

February 2021

JD sipped her tea. Pu-ehr blended green tea, her one true vice. An expensive blend, but it was worth every penny. This was her favorite time of day, watching the sun creep above the horizon, bringing light to the darkness around her.

No breakfast to cook. Johnathan and the boys were in Alaska enjoying the Boy Scout experience. The house was spotless. More thanks to Sophia, the housekeeper, than herself.

The red circle on her datebook kept pulling her back. So many things had transpired since a part of her heart stopped feeling. She loved Johnathan, although he loved her more. It was unspoken, but somehow, she knew he'd accepted that.

They'd celebrated fifteen years of marriage, and she'd given him three sons. Her world was complete, and she was happy. It had been years since she'd seen Derrick. *His decision,* she reminded herself. It must have been difficult for him when she married Johnathan and began having children. Maybe it was too much of a reminder of what he'd thrown away. Guilt, did he feel guilt or regret over what he'd done?

On paper, at least, Derrick had lost everything. The property that had been in his family for generations was now a housing development. The grand house on Lake Ella sold along with any other properties with his name on them. Beautiful places she'd never visit again; the pain was simply too great.

At the beginning of each month, an automatic payment funded Derrick's prison account. Mitch was funding the appeals. A last-minute stay was in the works, but there'd be none. Derrick, at one time, was a multi-millionaire with friends everywhere, but none of that would or could do any good tonight.

Over the years, Mitch had moved Derrick's millions from offshore accounts into legal businesses in her name. Derrick had promised to take care of her, and he'd kept his word. She'd never want for anything. She owed him so much but at the same time nothing.

JD chastised herself and shifted her thoughts to Johnathan, remembering making love before the trip. She felt her lips curve into a smile, running the encounter through her mind. He'd strolled into the bedroom with a grin she knew well. He'd closed and locked the door. "I want you to think about me while I'm away."

He'd unbuttoned her cotton shirt, slid it off her shoulders, and dropped it to the floor. "You're so beautiful." He ran his index finger across the rise of her breasts and kissed the throbbing vein in her neck. With skilled hands, the bra joined the blouse on the floor. "Take off your jeans." His voice, commanding, deep, and sensual, sent a ripple of awareness through her.

He walked around her before he spoke. "That's it, princess," he'd said, caressing her bare bottom with his fingertips before sitting on the footstool. "Over my knees now, JD." This time his voice rang with authority.

He'd spanked her; her bottom was still tender days

later. He'd not only spanked her; the man had made love to her until she was fighting to catch her breath.

Her cell phone buzzed—Johnathan. "Good morning, my love." She let the Southern charm accent her words. She knew it drove him crazy.

"How's my sexy wife today? Still thinking about me?"

"Oh yeah."

"Good." His tone shifted to serious. "Baby, you okay?"

"Sure." She fought the growing anxiety. She knew he understood.

"Anything I can do to help?"

"You are. It's good to hear your voice." She changed the subject, *cry later.* Her emotions were all over the map. "How are the boys?"

"Having a wonderful time. We caught salmon, and the boys cleaned them. Fresh fish is on the menu tonight."

"Did you get pictures?"

"Of course, check your email. Baby, you know I love you, right?"

"You only say that because I'm a judge, and you might need a favor," she replied and sipped her tea.

"Never hurts to kiss up to Madame Justice."

"I love you, too."

"I know. You going to the prison?" Johnathan asked.

"Yes. Things need to be said. It's been so long he might not want to see me." She could hardly raise her voice above a whisper.

"It was his choice. He told you not to visit. You've done everything you could, and the firm's fighting for a stay." His tone was patient and reassuring.

"You and I both know he's out of time. Benjamin says Derrick's ready for it to be over."

"I wish I was there to be with you." His voice was soothing.

"We agreed it was important for you to be with the boys. I need to do this alone. I'll put on my big-girl panties and deal with it," she said with a chuckle.

"Not the black lacy ones?"

She knew her husband was trying to take her mind off things, and she'd play along. "Of course, my love, and the matching bra. The ones you bought me in Italy."

"JD, that's not fair. You're making me hot as hell."

She licked her lips. "Think of me tonight in the shower. Remember what happened the night you gave me the lingerie."

"Oh, I remember. I couldn't walk the next day. Hell, I can't go back into the cabin now. I'll have to walk around and think about anything but you, or jump in the cold lake. Damn, I miss you."

"Well, now we're even. Monday, I had to take a pillow to sit on in court. My rear was a bit tender, thank you very much."

"You're going to be the death of me, JD."

JD laughed. "But you'll go smiling, my love."

His tone turned serious again. "Baby, call me when you leave the prison. I mean it. I know how much he hurt you."

"I will. Hug the boys for me. Tell them we'll talk tomorrow. Johnathan, I love you."

"I know, baby."

"Talk to you soon." She managed to say the words through the forming tears.

"Okay, love you, and I'll think about you in the shower."

She tried to settle but couldn't. She puttered in the garden, tried to read motions for an upcoming trial, walked along the lake, and even tried to nap. Somehow, with all her fiddling, the day passed.

It was time to see Derrick. There were things she needed to say. JD wanted to hear Derrick say he was responsible. Her conscience could be clear when at nine forty-five, they'd push the injections, and he'd take his last breath.

She took her time dressing and finally chose a modest navy blue dress. It showed nothing but at the same time accented her curves. She pinned up her hair and added ruby earrings. The only gift she still owned Derrick had given her. The rest had long ago been given away or donated to charity. She topped off the look with red lipstick, checked her appearance in the mirror, and headed out.

The drive from Tallahassee to Raiford took two and a half hours. It seemed strange to be at the prison. Derrick had been on death row for eighteen years and fourteen days.

JD watched the sun set and headed to Warden Miller's office. This visit had been years in the planning. As a judge, she knew where many metaphorical bodies were buried, and like Mitch, she too now held many people's secrets. She'd done her homework. It hadn't been *if* the warden's son Bishop would screw up in a big way, it was *when.*

With Bishop facing fifteen years in prison for sexual assault, JD negotiated a deal, using a third party, with the parents of the young woman. They'd been more anxious for money than justice, or the father was, and he controlled his wife. With many favors called in, JD would spend time with Derrick before the execution. He'd be handcuffed and shackled, but they'd be alone.

Even after all this time, she needed to see him. Make sure he understood how much she loved him, and the pain he'd caused. Did he understand he'd been her whole world, and it was never the same after his betrayal? JD needed to hear Derrick say he was responsible for his actions.

****

"JD." There was surprise and happiness in his voice. "They told me I had a visitor. I never guessed it was you."

"How are you?" She noted the dark circles around his eyes, his hair gray. He was thin and gaunt. She wanted to reach out and hold him.

"I'm as good as I can be, I guess." Derrick shrugged a shoulder. "How did you get in here alone?"

"I'm a judge. People owe me favors." *I made sure they owed me favors.*

"I saw it in the paper. Plus, Benjamin was beaming when he visited after your appointment ceremony. It's good to see you."

"I wasn't sure you'd want to see me."

"I always wanted to see you; it was difficult. I saw what our life should have been."

"You mean because I married Johnathan?"

"No. I'm glad you married Johnathan; he's a good man. Every time I saw you married, pregnant, and happy, it was like a knife to my gut. My choices took you from me; it's our life you're living with him. You loved me, and I screwed it up. This hell was a result of the choices

I made," he said, waving his hands.

JD leaned in. "I thought you hated me."

"No, it hurt too much. I'm glad you're here."

"Good, I wanted to talk to you."

"About what?"

"Clear the air. It's time." For a while, they talked about everything and nothing.

"Excuse me." Both looked up. "I'm Pastor Thompson."

"I'll give you a few minutes," JD whispered.

"JD, would you please stay?" Derrick asked.

As the man spoke and prayed, she reached across the table and placed her hand over Derrick's.

"Judge, you have ten minutes," the pastor said, checking his watch, and leaving the cell.

"Thank you," JD said. "Derrick, do you remember you told me there was one thing you wanted in our relationship?"

"Yes, total and complete honesty."

"You regulated how I dressed, how I acted. You molded me into the perfect woman you could show off and manipulate to make yourself look good. You never gave me a chance to see the other part of your life. Never talked to me or explained or tried to find a compromise. I would've done anything for you. You demanded complete honesty, yet you lied, cheated, and almost destroyed me."

His voice was urgent now. "JD, there isn't time to rehash that. It's important you understand I didn't murder Megan."

JD crossed her legs, took a deep breath, and slowly let it out. "From where I sit, there's a difference between the act of murder and being responsible for it."

"What are you talking about?"

JD stared at the institution-gray block wall, shook her head, and laughed. *Typical man, no clue.* Facing him again, she spoke, "I know you're innocent, but you are certainly responsible." JD read the confusion on his face before she checked her watch. *Only minutes left.*

"What are you talking about?"

"Remember the one thing I asked for in our relationship?"

He thought for a long minute. "Me being faithful? But what does that have to do with anything?"

She continued as if he hadn't spoken. "If you cheated, all bets were off, and you'd be responsible for the consequences."

"Yes."

JD read puzzlement on his face. She watched his thoughts spin, trying to put the pieces together. Her tone was low, sweet, and direct. "I discovered your lifestyle about a year before the murder. I went to the shed to get a screwdriver and found your box of toys."

She watched the color drain from his face. "I began my research. I'm very good at research. Hacking your email was easy. Didn't know I could do that, did you? You thought I was a computer idiot." JD bit back the burning anger she'd held in for years.

Derrick sat stone-faced, his mouth opening and closing like a fish.

"Anyway, that's not important." She waved her hand and continued, "I waited until you provided the perfect setup. I knew the security company employee would make a check around five, would see the open door, check it out, find the scene, and call the police."

She let herself smile just a bit. "I pretended to have

a migraine. You remember the awful migraines I'd been having for months? You acted concerned. 'Go home, turn off your phone,' you told me. 'Don't push so hard.' Like before, I followed the pattern you'd set.

"I know you have questions, but let me finish. You can ask them if there's time." She patted his hand.

"Getting out of the house was the first problem. Remember the window that kept setting off the alarm, or that's what I said. You disconnected it to stop bothering the security company. Gave me the perfect way to slip out and walk to Max's house.

"He'd left an extra set of keys while he was on sabbatical. You know the '68 Nova, no GPS, no trace of the trip. While you were at the hotel drinking with your whore, I put the tainted wine in the refrigerator.

"I used my own special mixture, all those herbs you encouraged me to grow, keep me busy while you were working—well, really out fucking everything that walked.

"The herbalism courses I took, and grew medicinal plants. Using that knowledge, I developed a perfect combination, a quick-acting sedative that showed up as a naturally occurring pathogen in the body."

"But—" Derrick tried to interrupt.

JD raised her hands and laughed. "Like I said, hold your questions to the end. I hid in the attic, you did the hard part, tying her to the bed with silk ties I gave you," she added, continuing to twist the knife. "Oh, and I wore a crime scene suit and gloves.

"When you both passed out, I used pictures from your safe as a model to make the small cuts on her body, then cuddled up behind you, put my hand over yours and stabbed her several times, and slit her throat. Sliced your hand, making sure there'd be a mixture of blood. The rest was easy. I replaced the tainted wine bottle and glasses. Pressed both of your hands on them to make sure your fingerprints would be found.

"I won't bore you with the minor details. I gathered up everything—computers, my clothing—replaced the tainted bottle of wine and glasses, and slipped out. You were passed out, so fingerprints were easy to put on the new items.

"The only loose end was Megan's computer and phone, and she brought them with her. I wiped the computer hard drives, stored them and the phones in a five-gallon bucket of paint in Max's garage with the other items. He was gone for a year; I had no trouble getting rid of the evidence later.

"I stopped on a back road, crushed and disposed of the wine bottles and glasses. You made it so easy. Questions?" she asked, relishing the delight in her voice.

"But you could never kill anyone." The words fumbled out as a whisper.

"You're the killer because you couldn't keep your dick in your pants or even be honest with me."

"You did all this—killing that woman, setting me up, marrying my best friend, having his children were all to hurt me and teach me a lesson?" Derrick asked.

JD smiled. "Yes."

"Derrick, it's time. Judge, you'll have to leave," the guard said.

"Wait a minute," Derrick almost yelled.

JD heard the pleading in his voice.

She whispered so only he could hear. "I loved you so much. What did you always say? 'Payback is a bitch.' And by the way, I love to be spanked. All you had to do was ask. Johnathan's a wonderful master."

Derrick was led down the hall. He looked back over his shoulder as he spoke in mumbles to the guard.

JD made her way to the waiting room. When the curtain rolled back, Derrick was strapped to the gurney. He said no last words, only stared at JD as a tear rolled down his cheek. She smiled when his body went limp and his eyelids were closed by the doctor. He was in Hell where he belonged.

JD exited the prison, climbed into her car, and hit speed dial number one. Johnathan answered on the first ring.

"Baby, you okay?"

She heard the concern in his voice. "Yes, never better. I said everything I've held in for years. He looked old and scared. It was awful for him to have suffered so long."

"Did he admit to the murder?"

"Of course not, but I know he's responsible."

"You've never said it before. I thought you believed he was innocent."

"Derrick, innocent?" She let out a laugh. "It was easier not to talk about it." After a pause, she continued, "Are you behaving yourself in the wilds of Alaska? No woman caught your fancy?"

He laughed. "You're the only woman I want and need."

"Good to hear. I'd be very unhappy if you found someone else to play."

"Never, my love. My goal in life is to keep you happy."

"Good, that's very good to know. I'll see you in a few days."

JD placed her cell phone on the seat. Derrick was in Hell, and maybe one day, she'd join him. But for now, she'd use justice to make all those cheating bastards pay. He was right about one thing: payback is a bitch.

A word about the author...

EJ Towler lives in coastal Virginia and enjoys writing tales of extraordinary women and the men they love or sometimes only tolerate. When not writing, EJ enjoys the roles of wife, sister, mother, grandmother, Army Veteran, and dachshund advocate.

She travels a great deal and finds ideas for books and short stories in everyday situations and her past. Her characters often won't do what she asks, so she acts as peacekeeper between and in the end, they find a way to co-exist.

Her writing companions are rescue dachshund Brownie, a 13-year-old frosty face senior who loves to cuddle, and her service dog Huckleberry Hound. Huck is a brindle dachshund who recently completed his service/medical alert dog training through Train A Dog Save A Warrior. Yes, dachshunds can be service dogs too.

Dachshunds are supporting characters to all EJ's heroines in hopes of bringing attention to rescue of this lovable breed who are two dogs long and half a dog high. A percentage of her royalties are donated to support various dachshund rescue groups.

http://ejtowler.com
@TowlerEJ
@Huckservicedog